WILD AND WANTON

Dorothy Vernon

CHIVERS
THORNDIKE

This Large Print book is published by BBC Audiobooks Ltd, Bath, England and by Thorndike Press®, Waterville, Maine, USA.

Published in 2004 in the U.K. by arrangement with the author.

Published in 2004 in the U.S. by arrangement with Juliet Burton Literary Agency.

U.K. Hardcover ISBN 1–4056–3069–8 (Chivers Large Print)
U.K. Softcover ISBN 1–4056–3070–1 (Camden Large Print)
U.S. Softcover ISBN 0–7862–6865–4 (Nightingale)

The text of this Large Print edition is unabridged.
Other aspects of the book may vary from the original edition.

Set in 16 pt. New Times Roman.

Printed in Great Britain on acid-free paper.

British Library Cataloguing in Publication Data available

Library of Congress Control Number: 2004107819

Chapter One

'Nick Farraday wants six young blondes,' Jim Bourne announced, recognizing the soft step that approached his desk.

'That shouldn't present a problem. All he has to do is crook his finger and any number will come running,' Lindsay Cooper said dryly.

'How did someone as young as you get to be such a cynic?' her employer rebuked, but his tone was as soft as the thoughts flitting under his thick gray thatch of hair.

Lindsay's hair was blond, soft and fly-away, its wayward strands trapped at the back of her slender neck in a narrow ribbon. If he'd been ten years younger he would have reached out before now and untied that small, neat, black velvet bow.

Jim Bourne remembered when he'd first interviewed her for the position of his secretary. It had been one of those days when everything goes wrong, and he had been elbow-deep in work. He had desperately wanted someone to take the mountain of paperwork off his hands, a mountain getting higher because of the time he was wasting on interviewing unsuitable applicants.

'Sit down. Be with you in a moment,' he'd growled.

He had liked the way she sat so patiently,

with no nervous twisting of fingers. Her hands had rested quietly on her lap, and he had detected a trace of shyness in the way her eyes had been fixed upon them. Her long lashes, obligingly colored by nature a darker gold than her hair, were still casting silky shadows on her cheeks when he'd eventually gotten round to giving her his attention.

'And now, Miss Cooper. Tell me a little about yourself.'

The next second he'd found himself dazzled by the amazing beauty of her eyes—not blue, as he would have expected from her fair coloring, but a deep and rich tawny gold. Qualifications hadn't seemed important anymore. He would have engaged her for her eyes alone. Yet she wasn't a beauty, not by any stretch of the imagination, and her figure, though quite easy on the eye, could not claim to have a model's statistics. She had a tiny waist, with soft curves above and below. Fashion trends favored the snake-hipped, long-legged look which she lacked, although the shape of her legs was more than just okay. He knew about these things, indeed considered himself to be something of an expert, since he ran one of London's most successful modeling agencies—hence the reason Nick Farraday, of the House of Delmar, had come to him for six blondes.

'When I say he wants six blondes, that's just a round figure. He'll select one from the bunch we send over. It's all very hush-hush, but in the absolute confidence that it will go no further than these four walls, I can tell you it's got to do with a new product that will be marketed under the trade name of Allure. The woman selected for the promotion is going to be one lucky beauty. Overnight fame, and all the trimmings that go with it, will be hers.'

Lindsay tried to look suitably impressed, even though such things didn't cut much ice with her.

She must have succeeded; at least her expression elicited a satisfied nod from her employer as he continued. 'Naturally, as you'd imagine, Farraday being the head of a large cosmetic house, the girls must have flawless complexions. The only other stipulation he made is coloring. I understand this has to complement the gold-and-white packaging. Do we have six blondes available for instant call?'

'How instant?'

'Day after tomorrow. Evening.'

Two whom Lindsay might have called on were out of the country. Another very popular model was on an assignment in Leeds and not due back until the middle of the next week. 'No, but—' This time the dry inflection in her voice was rooted in sincerity—'for Nick Farraday, every girl on call will make an appointment with her hair stylist.'

A slight frown shifted Jim Bourne's lips. 'Farraday won't stand being cheated, and he has an astute eye.'

'People who cheat themselves are usually like that. Aware of all the angles.'

'Do you know the guy?'

'Only by repute.'

'That's not always a reliable source. Even if only half of what has been said about Farraday was true, he would have to be . . .' He coughed, and an abashed grin curved his mouth. 'I'll spare your blushes. In case evening work causes a problem, since I know it's not too popular with a girl who has an assignment for the following morning, I'll throw in another carrot. The venue is Nick Farraday's penthouse suite.' His grin widened at the quickening of interest on Lindsay's face. 'That even intrigues you. I bet you'd rearrange your own plans to get an eyeful of his *reputedly* sumptuous lifestyle,' he said, unable to resist the gibe.

'Don't kid yourself,' Lindsay retorted, getting briskly to her feet. 'It's short notice. I'd better get busy.'

Smiling slyly, not the least bit fooled by her feigned lack of interest, Jim said, 'If you can only rustle up five blondes, you can be the sixth yourself.'

She made a face at him. 'It would serve you right if I did, and Nick Farraday chose me.'

'Lindsay, you're a honey, but . . .'

'I know, no chance of catching his eye.' At the same time a speculative look entered the tawny gold depths of her own eyes. 'Would you mind if I took you up on what you just said and went along? Just for the fun of it.' Why she added that she didn't know. Even as quick as Jim was, he couldn't know what her real motive was. She wanted only to observe, not be observed in the hope that Nick Farraday would take a fancy to her.

Nick Farraday, and the elite, glittery circle he revolved in, were as far removed from her life as it was possible to be. And that was the way she wanted it to stay. She knew that that put her in a minority; most women were fascinated by the mere mention of his name. But when she thought of Nick Farraday, her reaction was one of revulsion. In her opinion, the women who lit up for him, angling for his attention and hoping to be added to his list of conquests, were a disgrace to their sex. They did not seem to mind knowing that once they were elevated to the exalted rank of paramour they could start counting the days until his jaded eye strayed in search of another eager victim. It was said that he was very generous when it came to the pay-off. With his vast wealth he could afford to be. But there were some things which no amount of money could buy, at least in Lindsay's mind.

Grinning widely, Jim said, 'Is that an admission that I'm right and you're as curious as anyone to see the great man up close?'

There was more to it than that. An excited

5

shiver of apprehension ran down her spine, as if she could pierce the shrouds that concealed the future and somehow see beyond them. Jim could think what he liked as long as it got her a chance to see the demon in his den.

Her mouth tilted upward at each corner. There was something infectious and beguiling about the smile that lifted her winsome face into a completely different category, almost one of beauty. 'Don't tell me it's just a feminine characteristic. Wouldn't you like to curl up on the window seat and take a surreptitious peep from behind the plush velvet drapes?'

'How do you know that his drapes are velvet, or that there's a window seat, for that matter?' Jim inquired, a shrewd, concerned frown creasing his forehead.

'I must have read it somewhere. Maybe one of the glossies did a feature on his home,' she invented quickly.

Jim accepted that, but she knew that it had been a most indiscreet slip and that she would have to guard her tongue in the future. If he thought there was anything, anything at all, plaguing her about Nick Farraday, he would block her attempt to see him.

She knew all about Jim Bourne's feelings for her, how strongly he was attracted to her. Several times she had sensed that he was tempted to put their relationship on a different footing. She even knew why he hadn't made a move in that direction. His prematurely gray hair made him look older than he was, but even at forty-two he considered himself too old for her. In terms of worldly experience she realized that they were separated by more than the actual twenty years' difference. He had come up the hard way—he had been on his own since he was sixteen, and even before that he had gotten used to taking his knocks. Anyone who had pulled himself up from nothing had to have a streak of ruthlessness in his makeup. And guts. And those characteristics had overflowed into his personal life. He had played as hard as he'd worked, but now he was ready to settle down. Perhaps he hadn't settled down before because he had never met a woman for whom he had the right kind of feelings, but that had backfired on him, in a sense: it was the very tender, protective nature of his regard for Lindsay that was holding him back. He thought she should find a mate of her own sort, someone who hadn't yet tasted all the fruits of life.

Lindsay had never properly analyzed her feelings toward him, which were reciprocal—up to a point. She was most certainly attracted to his looks. He had a friendly, lived-in face, and brown eyes that induced a feeling of trust. His build and physique could be described as better than average. And his gray hair was not a detriment to his appearance, but a distinguishing feature. *He* was the one who was careful not to brush too close; she never bothered to guard against it. She had once asked herself if she would back away if he made a pass at her, and in all honesty hadn't been able to come up with an answer.

'Well?' she beseeched softly. 'Is it all right if I put my own name down?'

'Of course. Just go easy on the liquor. Remember, you haven't much of a head for it.'

'Liquor?' she queried.

'Did I forget to mention it? Farraday's throwing a party. Looks, apparently, aren't all that he wants. Intelligence, intellect, and personality also count. He wants to observe the models, see how they shape up in public, how at ease they are with people, and vice versa. It's not enough for her appeal to be drawn out by a clever cameraman; she's got to radiate it.'

Defensively Lindsay said, 'Most of the girls on our books do, so there's no problem there. But . . . intellect, did you say?'

'I know. That might present difficulties.'

'If I'd said that it would have sounded catty.'

'That's why I said it for you.'

'Thanks. It's nice to have someone going on ahead and dethorning the roses for me. Do you know, I can only think of four girls who meet all the requirements.'

'Besides yourself?'

'Of course. You wouldn't like to put on a

blond wig and come in drag, would you?'

'Out!'

She left on the double, leaving behind the delicious sound of his laughter.

She spent much of what was left of the day on the telephone. Her endeavors paid off, and she knew by day's end that she could count on five of the loveliest girls in the modeling profession. Moreover, she had accomplished her task with only a minimum of cheating. She had advised one girl to remember to smile and say as *little* as possible. And then, with an even greater fear of being chastised later, she had whispered the words 'blonde rinse' to another.

That evening, going through her wardrobe while thinking about the competition she would face, she wondered what Nick Farraday would think of the cuckoo in the nest. It would have been easy to make the competition less weighted against herself, but she hadn't; rather, she had been scrupulously honest in her selection. A frown tormented her forehead as she wondered where that thought had come from. She wasn't in competition: she was going for personal reasons, not as a possible applicant. Still, it was feminine to want to look her best.

Her wardrobe was less than helpful; she had not one dress that was even remotely suitable. So the next day she gave herself an extended lunch break and went shopping.

After more than two years she still caught

her breath at the beauty of London's churches, designed by such well-known names as Sir Christopher Wren and James Gibbs. The Gothic cathedrals, Victorian grandeur and Georgian elegance, Regency terraces and Renaissance palaces, and pageantry that was positively medieval in its splendour—all delighted her heart and eyes. She could never exhaust the sightseeing possibilities of the parks and art galleries and museums. She loved to watch the changing of the guard at Buckingham Palace, and the Horse Guards Parade. She loved the Cockney warmth of the cab drivers, loved the ballet and the opera and the maze of theatres. After dark, Shaftesbury Avenue turned into a glittering wonderland. And the shops! They were a whole fascination in themselves! They ranged from Harrods, the domed brownstone palace that was Knightsbridge's chief landmark, and Fortnum & Mason in Piccadilly, to the street markets and the shops in Oxford Street and Regent Street, more within Lindsay's modest means.

In coming to London she'd followed her brother, Phil, who had raved in his letters about the new life he'd made for himself. He'd said that it was like being reborn. Of course, Cathy, the girl he'd met in London and married after a whirlwind courtship, could have added to the enchantment.

City life had taken some getting used to for a girl whose roots had been in a small stone village in the north of England. There were still occasions when Lindsay felt a tremendous sense of awe, but for the most part she'd adapted well; London was now her city. At first it had seemed like a dream, but now her past was the dream and this was the reality. Though she'd been lucky in her job and now earned a good salary, the luxury of having her own apartment made making ends meet a problem.

Ami, one of the models, had told her about a trendy boutique in King's Road which featured high fashion at low prices, a veritable paradise for anyone on a tight budget who needed to look good. It seemed an appropriate time to find out if Ami had been right.

She gave herself over completely to the salesgirl and was guided into buying a figure-clinging black sheath of a gown that accentuated the lovely curves of her figure as well as her fair coloring and pale blond hair. Because of an imperfection that was barely noticeable, and then only if pointed out, the gown came at a fraction of its intended price. It was the kind of gown that went with French perfume and Russian sable. Even without those luxurious extras Lindsay felt very desirable and expensive in it—not at all herself. Since she had no appropriate footwear she had to make a second purchase—high-heeled black sandals with a silver thread enhancing delicate straps. This color scheme would enhance her silver bracelet and necklace, the only really good jewelry she possessed.

When she tried everything on again back at her apartment she was quite shocked to see what a sensuous image she cut. She hadn't realized how daring the dress was. But because it was too late to do anything about it now, she valiantly tried to swallow her apprehension.

The arrangement was for each model to make her own way to Nick Farraday's penthouse suite. Since they all lived in different sections of the city, this was the sensible course, but on leaving the friendly confines of the London taxicab that evening she felt oddly isolated. She wished she had someone with her for support as she entered the elevator which connected directly with the penthouse. On stepping out again she found herself looking at another door. It hadn't occurred to her that the penthouse would be sound-proofed, and the lack of noise coming from the suite made her wonder if she had come to the wrong address, particularly because she wasn't conspicuously early.

On the door was a button that she assumed was attached to a bell. She pressed it. The door glided open, and a glittery, noisy scene exploded before her astonished eyes. The party was really going with a bang. A maid approached, looking very chic in her uniform, and showed Lindsay to the ladies' powder

12

room, first taking her coat from her and hanging it up. A last cursory glance in the mirror did nothing to calm the misgivings that were crowding back. She was worried about the dress, and wondered whether leaving her hair loose, as the salesgirl had recommended, was appropriate. Did it make her look a little wild and wanton? Should she be there at all? She asked herself. What was the purpose? She was stirring up an old sadness, making herself desperately unhappy all over again.

A man in his mid to late thirties came forward to greet her. He stood about five eight or nine, and had light brown hair that was beginning to recede. Though he had a homely face, he looked friendly, and Lindsay warmed to him even before he announced his name.

'Greg Hammond,' he said easily, extending his hand. 'I'm happy to welcome you.'

'Lindsay Cooper.' As she gave her own name she responded to his friendliness with a smile.

Cathy had talked a lot about Greg Hammond. He had been supportive at the time of Phil's death, and to the best of Lindsay's knowledge he and Cathy still kept in touch. All the same, her tongue had locked momentarily before giving her surname as she wondered if he would connect her with Phil. She knew that he had been her brother's friend as well as a colleague at work.

To her intense relief nothing showed on his face as he said, 'You're from the modeling agency, right?'

'How very astute of you to know that!' She could have said 'How amazing!' but because models tended to have a certain polish which she knew she lacked, she decided on the more formal response.

His 'astute' remark was neatly explained when he said, 'Not really. I know it looks to be a select crowd here this evening, but most of them are regulars. I've been in Nick Farraday's employ long enough to be acquainted with all the people he knows. Besides,' he added with a puckish smile, 'I compiled the guest list.'

'That does give you something of an advantage.' Her smile subsided slightly as she inquired, 'Isn't Mr. Farraday here?'

She had never met Nick Farraday, though she had formulated an image of how he'd look. Her eyes momentarily left Greg Hammond's face to scan the throng in an attempt to find someone who matched this image. But she couldn't see anyone wearing horns.

She thought it was rude of her host not to be present to receive his guests in person. Except, she remembered, she wasn't a guest in the conventional sense, merely there to be looked over as a possible Miss Allure.

'He's around,' Greg Hammond announced airily. 'He'll single you out when he's ready.

Meanwhile, just mix naturally and enjoy yourself.'

'Could you, knowing you were being spied on?'

'That's coming it a bit heavy, isn't it? This is an extremely important assignment, and a most lucrative one for the right girl. A pretty face and spot-on statistics aren't enough. It's essential to see how the prospective choice makes out in public. But surely you were briefed about this before you came? So why the resentment? Do you know Mr. Farraday?'

'No.'

'So what gives with you?' Greg Hammond asked, his tone equable and friendly, but getting it across to Lindsay that he wouldn't take kindly to criticism of his boss.

There was a temporary pause while Greg Hammond stopped a circulating waiter, and the conversation wasn't resumed until a plate was in Lindsay's hand and she had made her selections from the tempting canapes on the tray.

'You can't take up cudgels against a man you don't know. You weren't having me on about that?'

'No, I've never met Nick Farraday. That's not to say, however, that I haven't heard a lot about him.'

That slipped out before she could help it, and Greg Hammond gave a long, drawn-out sigh of comprehension. 'I see!' he exclaimed.

15

A second waiter was stopped, and Lindsay selected a glass of champagne. So did Greg. He raised his glass to his lips. 'Here's to you. Now, where were we? Ah, yes! I was just about to do some gentle probing into the obvious aversion you have for Mr. Farraday, a man you assure me you have never met. That being so, he can't have wronged you personally, so this antipathy must be on someone else's behalf. May I speak frankly?'

Regretting her runaway tongue, and squirming in dismay, Lindsay had no option but to say, 'Feel free.'

But it was not to be. His candid speaking was cut off as a hand tapped him on the shoulder and a deep, attractive, masculine voice informed him, 'You're wanted over there.' She didn't know whether she was delighted to be let off, or annoyed at having her curiosity frustrated, because despite her uneasiness it would have been interesting to hear what Greg Hammond had to say.

'Sure.' Shrugging, Greg Hammond smiled into Lindsay's eyes. 'It's always the same when I find myself alone with a pretty girl. See you around!' he concluded jauntily before taking off. Obviously, when Nick Farraday cracked the whip people jumped to attention.

Lindsay was conscious of the fact that the man who had delivered the summons that sent Greg Hammond speeding away had elected to stay by her side. In the circles she moved in,

16

with models getting taller, she was used to women as well as men towering over what she had previously considered to be a respectable height. At five feet five inches, no one could have called her pint-sized, but that was how she suddenly felt as she tilted her head back in order to look at him.

He was expensively dressed. The impeccable cut of his dinner jacket whispered very discreetly that it was tailor-made; the wafer-thin watch on his wrist was gold, his shoes Italian. He was obviously one of the elite and excessively well-paid members of Nick Farraday's staff. The breadth of his shoulders and the almost aggressive stance of his muscular legs provided Lindsay with a possible clue to his identity. Men as wealthy as Nick Farraday were vulnerable. She had noticed that this suite was guarded by a full security system, but he no doubt also needed a full-time bodyguard, and she made the snap decision that the position was adequately filled by this man.

Lindsay had two shortcomings that frequently landed her in delicate situations. One was her predilection for making snap judgments. The other was that she saw only what she wanted to see. Afterward, in playing the scene over again in her mind, she knew that this was yet another instance of hopeful thinking on her part, and that somewhere deep down in her a voice had been telling her

17

this man was Nick Farraday. She could not admit this to herself and at the same time acknowledge the impact he made on her—an instant, electric attraction, like nothing she had ever before experienced. So she had to fool herself about his identity. She couldn't bear for him to be the man against whom she bore a fierce grudge. Hence, she dismissed the notion that he might be Nick Farraday before it had a chance to take hold of her.

His hair was black, his eyes the startling blue of a tropical sky. How well they went with a complexion that could only have achieved its attractive shade of bronze under a tropical sun. His physique was as outrageously handsome and as eye-catching as his face. Never in the whole of her life had she mentally stripped a man, but she suddenly saw this one reclining on white sand, his lean hips encased in white swimming trunks that showed off his spectacular suntan.

'I didn't think Greg had said enough to make you blush. The . . . interesting part was still to come when I butted in. You've either heard the rest of the story before, or you've got a very athletic mind.'

She would much rather he knew *anything* than that the blush that had risen to her cheeks was because of her thoughts about him. Swallowing to regain her composure, she queried, 'Athletic?'

'Capable of making long jumps and landing

dead on target. I don't usually eavesdrop, but I must confess that on this occasion I found the nature of the conversation too irresistible to pass up.'

'And you know what Mr. Hammond was getting at?'

'I'm sure he would prefer you to call him Greg, but stay with Mr. Hammond. Yes, unfortunately I think I do. You've never met Nick Farraday.' He wasn't asking her, he was telling her. 'That's what you said.'

'Yes.' She was finding it difficult to unlock her gaze from the compelling force of his eyes.

'So it's secondhand hate, the worst kind,' he said scathingly. 'Hating on behalf of someone else should carry a warning because rarely are all the circumstances disclosed by the party on whose behalf the hating is done. That's natural enough, because who wants to lose face with someone who cares enough about you to spring to your defense?'

'The fact that you've got all this down pat must mean that it's a regular occurrence,' Lindsay said, her voice less searing than it might have been because of her blocked breath.

His shrug could have meant anything. 'The women who are favored never have anything to complain about. It has happened that someone near and dear to someone out of favor, a close relative or a friend, has attempted to inveigle her way in, wearing the

19

kind of dress that excites a man's eye, but with a heart full of revenge beating in the breast so tantalizingly . . .' His eyes took over and were as eloquent as his tongue as they followed the course of the silver chain suspended round her neck; it was a look as warm as a caress as it dipped to the neckline of her dress.

The dress hadn't seemed so low-cut when she'd tried it on in the shop. Because the back was slashed even more daringly; it wasn't possible to wear a bra with it, though the bodice had a strip of double-facing. The concentration of his gaze made her extremely grateful for that. She wondered what setting he had used for her in his mind. A sickle of white sand . . . or the silk sheets of a bed?

His eyes returned to her face, and only then did she manage to get command of herself. 'Is that what Mr. Hammond thought? Did he think I was rising to the defense of a friend who had . . . I don't quite know how to put this.'

'Served her usefulness and been dropped?' he supplied for her.

'Yes, that's what I mean.'

'But in your case, that's not so?' he queried speculatively.

'No. I've heard stories about Nick Farraday's amorous entanglements. Who hasn't?'

His smile turned wry. 'Sometimes I think that on dull, no-news days the media says to itself, let's find out what Nick Farraday is up to. But I'm straying from the point. If you aren't personally acquainted with a woman who has given her favors and ceased to amuse, why the intense dislike of Nick Farraday?'

He was easy to talk to, and she hadn't realized how obvious she had been. Her hatred of Nick Farraday for his part in her brother's downfall and eventual death was so deep that it was almost an intrinsic part of her, something so accepted that she'd felt no need to cover it up. But she wasn't here for revenge; that wasn't her style. She had no devious plot in her mind. She had just wanted to see for herself what manner of man Nick Farraday was. And perhaps she had been curious to see if his apartment was as luxurious as Phil had described it to her in his letters. Her wish had been granted, and she now saw that the apartment did indeed live up to her brother's rave reviews.

'Why the antagonism?' he repeated when no reply seemed forthcoming.

She searched for the words that would let her answer within the bounds of truth, but without giving anything away. 'I suppose I dislike him because it doesn't seem right for one man to have so much.'

'Him?' The query had a teasing inflection. 'Ah . . . yes!' Something about his smile disturbed her. 'Have you never coveted wealth?'

21

'Never!' she declared emphatically.

'I find that hard to believe. What are your interests?'

'I don't know what that's got to do with what we're talking about, but I'll answer anyway. I like reading and music.'

'And you have never wished to possess any particular, expensive book? You have never yearned with all your heart to be sitting in one of the highest-priced seats at some much-acclaimed performance? Have you never wished you could donate an expensive piece of equipment to a hospital, or fill a hungry child's stomach in some far-off, deserted corner of the world?'

'Of course I have!' she replied testily, caring for neither the strange effect he had on her nor the turn of the conversation:

'Then you *have* coveted wealth, because these things, whether desired for personal pleasure or from noble intent, have the same thing in common: both require money.'

'You have a clever tongue. I imagine you could talk your way out of a prison.'

'I've done a lot of things in my time, willingly and unwillingly, but that has never been asked of me.'

Her mind backtracked. 'What did you mean by the . . . er . . . interesting part?' she ventured delicately.

'What interesting part?' The line of his mouth was suspiciously straight. Was he teasing her?

'When you butted in just now, you said you didn't think that Mr. Hammond had said enough to make me blush because he hadn't got to the interesting part.'

He *had* been teasing her, because he came back with, 'I didn't think you'd let that one drop. I'm quite prepared to tell you what I'm certain Greg was about to say. But first I must remind you that you'd given Greg permission to speak frankly.'

'So I had! I'd forgotten about that. Perhaps you'd better not tell me.'

Her lowered eyes came up again when she heard him say, 'Would you have me break my golden rule?'

'What golden rule?'

'Never to leave a woman unsatisfied.' Her flush at the sensual undertone deepened as he added, 'Would you have me deny your burning curiosity?'

'No,' she croaked.

'We're back to the scorned woman bit. Not the woman herself—she knew the score—but someone who feels she's justified in feeling hurt and anger on behalf of someone she is fond of. It's my belief that Greg was going to point out that there can be no justification for that kind of reaction by acquainting you with a fact so basic that you shouldn't need to be told: It always takes two. And I can go one better than Greg. Nick Farraday has his faults, and no one is in a position to know that better than I, but taking a woman to his bed who needs to be tutored on the finer points is something he does *not* have on his conscience. I can vouch for the truth of that.'

Only one man could 'vouch for the truth of that,' and that was Nick Farraday himself. There was an outcry in her head, a protest that splintered to pierce the bubble of excitement that had been steadily rising within her at being in the company of this magnetic man. The disappointment was as acute as her sharply indrawn breath, and a hundred times more painful.

'You must have found this all very amusing ... Mr. Farraday!'

She wasn't surprised. You could only fool yourself for so long. It had been there all the time, a blighting shadow of thought pressing ever closer, telling her that she wasn't in the company of Nick Farraday's bodyguard, but the man himself!

Oddly enough, he didn't suddenly grow horns, as her image of him had dictated he should. The mesmeric voice was as smooth as ever as he continued. 'Even rakes have a code of honor. A gentleman must never introduce the pleasures of womanhood to an innocent girl unless his intentions are as pure as she is. It's a code I have had no difficulty in adhering to. But then, perhaps that's because curious minds in eager young bodies are like ... gold dust,' he said, reaching out and touching the pale gold of her hair.

'You could have told me who you are,' she said, jerking away from his fingers.

'I didn't set out to deceive you. Who did you think I was?'

'A bodyguard.'

'I haven't got one. Never felt the need.'

'Such assurance has a very arrogant ring to it. Aren't you afraid that one day someone will attempt to harm you, Mr. Farraday?'

'I'll take my chances. And the name's Nick. I don't recall catching your name.'

'Lindsay Cooper,' she submitted frostily, searching his face as keenly as she had searched Greg Hammond's to see if he remembered that Phil's name had been Cooper and was making a connection.

It was her first name he meditated over. 'Lindsay,' he said, rolling it softly over his tongue. 'The name is almost as alluring as you are.' He put his head to one side and looked at her through narrowed eyes. He was studying her almost as an artist would. 'Yes,' he said. 'Indeed, very . . . *alluring*.'

Why the hesitation? Why the emphasis? Why *alluring*? What was going on in his head? What did it mean? It was surely just coincidental usage of a word. He wasn't looking at her as the Allure girl. What she'd said to Jim Bourne about being chosen by Nick Farraday had been a joke. She had as much

25

chance of being selected Miss Allure as she had of flapping her arms and finding that she could fly.

Chapter Two

Without warning or explanation, Nick Farraday grabbed hold of her and propelled her across the room.

'Where are you taking me?' Lindsay demanded, hoping the alarm she felt hadn't crept into her voice as she struggled to free her wrist from his fingers. They reached a door, and it became apparent to her that they were going through it. 'Mr. Farraday,' she implored, 'you can't walk out on your own party.'

'I'm the host; I can do what I want. And I thought I told you, the name is Nick. Mr. Farraday sounds too prim.'

'I *am* prim,' she retaliated furiously, wondering how he was managing to abduct her, as it were, why no one offered to stop him. It must have been obvious that she was being dragged out against her will. Two possible reasons for this general apathy occurred to her. Either no one questioned Nick Farraday's actions, or, in this crush, no one had noticed their exit. She supposed she could have screamed, but that seemed undignified, and although he was acting outrageously, she

26

didn't really think he had any evil intentions. She changed her mind rapidly when she found herself being pushed into a bedroom.

Not *his* bedroom, she surmised, unless he liked soft pink lamps and frilly drapes. She wasn't given the chance to see more than that, because she was immediately dragged into an adjacent dressing room. Still keeping her imprisoned with one hand, he used the other to open the door of a closet. After rifling through its contents impatiently, he drew out a white dress. Holding it out to her, he said, 'Put this on.'

'I will not!'

'Sorry, did I forget to say please?'

'You could get down on your knees, and the answer would be the same.'

'Then don't put it on. Just take off the dress you're wearing. And I'm not unaware of what you can't possibly be wearing underneath.'

'Just what kind of man are you?'

'One who's losing his patience.'

'*You* are? I should have thought that was *my* right. I'm not staying here to be ordered around in this indecent way.'

'You've got it all wrong. I'm just trying to point out that you'd look more decent naked than in the dress you've got on at the moment. Haven't you any idea how you look, or should I say *what* you look?'

'Even if I do look like what you're implying, you don't have to act upon it.'

'I'm not!'

'I'm too much of a lady to tell you what I think you are. I'm getting out of here. Fast.'

'The girl is right. I would leave if I were in her place.' This new voice came from the bedroom. A woman's voice, which even to Lindsay's astonished ear seemed to carry the delicacy of illness.

Lindsay's breath left her in a rush of relief as the hands that had seemed bent on ripping her black dress off her back suddenly loosened their hold. Nick Farraday called out, 'I thought you were asleep. I was going to wake you when I'd talked her into putting on something more suitable.'

'I hardly thought you were going to seduce the poor girl in my dressing room. And you can have no idea what these eyes have seen. In any case, I prefer to judge for myself, so bring her forward this instant to be introduced.'

'You heard,' Nick Farraday said to Lindsay in resignation as he swept her back into the bedroom.

'Nearer, child,' the voice that had summoned them instructed. As Nick's hand released her, Lindsay hesitated several feet from the gilded four-poster bed.

There was comfort in the realization that, as Lindsay now discovered, the voice wasn't delicate because of some temporary affliction, but because of the age of the speaker.

Looked down upon by painted cherubs,

propped up against a mound of silk pillows that bore the very famous monogram *L. D.*, for Luisa Delmar, founder of the House of Delmar, was a very old lady. Nick's grandmother must have been in her eighties, yet her skin was as smooth as porcelain, and as white, save for the delicate tint of pink in her cheeks. Her eyes were a shrewd and penetrating blue, not the tropical blue of Nick Farraday's, but the blue of an English sky. Her face was surrounded by a mass of baby-fine, silky white curls. She wore a pink silk, quilted bedjacket with her monogram exquisitely embroidered on the pocket. Her hands, all that gave away her advanced age, reposed tranquilly upon the bedcovers and were heavy with rings. Her swollen fingers gave evidence of rheumatic pain, and Lindsay wondered if the rings ever came off.

The woman held out one hand to Lindsay, who, for two reasons, was afraid to take it in greeting. In the first place, she was in awe of meeting such a great lady. And secondly, she was fearful that all but the lightest clasp would cause pain. Hence, she was delightedly surprised by the steely grip she encountered. Then Luisa Delmar bid her to turn round.

This done, with Lindsay all too aware of the sparkle in Nick's tropical-blue eyes, she had to swallow to meet the paler ones of his grandmother.

'Mmmmm. Pity you aren't taller. On the

other hand, you do have the grace of movement which height brings, and you're all there in the right places. Nick has an unfortunate and most infuriating habit of invariably being right. Who backed you into that dress? The color is fantastic, the perfect foil for your fairness. But the style! Oh, my dear!' Luisa said, shuddering delicately.

'Never mind the dress,' Nick Farraday instructed. 'Remove it from the body in your mind and then tell me that you don't see what I see.'

A dry chuckle found its way up the old woman's throat. 'Dear boy, I'm positive that I don't see what you see.'

'Don't be naughty, Luisa,' he said turning to Lindsay, Nick Farraday further admonished, 'Don't encourage her.'

'How am I encouraging her?' Lindsay gasped.

'By blushing.'

'Wouldn't you blush if someone mentally stripped you?'

'I doubt it very much. Did I?'

Damn him! Lindsay's blush deepened as she remembered how she had envisioned him in swim-trunks against a backdrop of white sand and blue sky.

'What are you mumbling about?' Luisa Delmar demanded querulously. 'You know my ears aren't as good as they used to be. Speak up!'

'Don't count on that,' Nick Farraday counseled Lindsay in a wicked aside before turning back to the bed. 'Yes, Luisa. Now, look at Lindsay and see it. Woman awakening. The bud about to blossom. You've got to agree that she's perfect.'

'Mmmmm,' Luisa Delmar said.

A vibrant note of excitement entered Nick Farraday's voice. 'Can't you feel that . . . allure? It's there, I tell you!'

'I see the possibility. Don't rush me; you know I like to take my time. I'm still disturbed by what you're seeing. I'm not convinced that you aren't looking at the girl on a more personal level.'

'Rubbish! You're creating difficulties where none exist.'

'Am I, Nick?' Looking at Lindsay, Luisa Delmar said, 'You must think us very rude, talking over your head as we are. Sit down, here on the edge of my bed. That's better,' she added as Lindsay obeyed. 'Now we're cozier. As you see, I'm having my own private party.' She waved a beringed hand at the nightstand, which contained food and champagne. 'A glass of champagne for Lindsay and something for her to eat,' she instructed Nick Farraday, 'and I will try to explain. But before I begin, I must ask two things of you, Lindsay. One, even though I don't intend to tell you much at this stage, things that may mean little to you would mean more to our competitors, and months of

31

planning, not to mention the expense involved, would come to nothing. So, anything you hear must remain behind sealed lips. Have I your promise?'

'Yes, Madame.'

'Good. The second thing I ask—no, command—is your absolute honesty. Have I got that, too?'

'That's easily granted. One of my failings is that I'm often too honest.'

'Yes, that *can* be a failing,' the old lady observed wryly.

'Champagne and something to nibble at,' Nick Farraday said, pressing a glass and a plate into Lindsay's hands.

Lindsay didn't want anything to eat, and she was intoxicated enough by events, but Luisa Delmar had decreed that she must have these things, and she wasn't brave enough to refuse. She didn't think anyone, including Nick Farraday, would dare to disobey this fascinating lady. She took a sip from her glass and the interrogation began.

At first Luisa Delmar followed the usual line of questioning an applicant for any kind of job could expect. Where did she live? What were her interests? Was she prepared to travel? Lindsay answered like someone in a trance, refusing to believe this was happening to her, giving Luisa Delmar the blind obedience the elderly woman had come to expect as her right.

'Are you committed to anyone, child? By that I mean, do you have a lover?' Perceiving the blush touching Lindsay's cheeks, she said, 'I should explain that I use the word lover the way it was meant in my day. So, do you have a manfriend?'

'No.'

'How old are you?'

'Twenty-two.'

All Lindsay's other replies had been favorably received, but this one was met with a frown. 'It's no good!' She tossed an angry look beyond Lindsay's head to Nick Farraday. 'In my day, yes! Today, seventeen would be suspect, but you know we agreed on nineteen, Nick, and a naive nineteen-year-old at that.'

'*You* said; I didn't agree,' Nick replied. 'A giddy teenager would be equally impossible. We need someone who has reached the age of poise and inner tranquility. Admittedly, I thought she was younger. I thought she was a little girl playing at being a woman.' Then Nick Farraday scowled at Lindsay, as if it were her fault that her parents hadn't waited another three years before having her! The bubble of humor rising in her made her wonder if she ought to apologize for her parents' lack of patience.

'It doesn't make any difference,' Nick Farraday announced abruptly. 'I tell you, she *is*.'

'Don't be ridiculous!' Luisa Delmar chided.

A gleam of wickedness entered her eyes as she said, 'I might be a doddering old woman who forgets day-to-day happenings, but there are things I can instantly recall. I know that while it is possible for you to know that she *isn't*, you can't claim to know the opposite.'

'You're not a doddering old woman, you're a wicked old woman, and this business of forgetting things is all a pretense to get attention. I tell you that I *do* know. A man can tell these things.'

'Stuff and nonsense! A woman needs only a minimal amount of intelligence to hoodwink a man at any time, and particularly about that. Don't you agree, Lindsay?'

'I don't know,' Lindsay said, trembling in her elegant sandals at daring to contest this imperious lady, and feeling her stomach sink as apprehension at what she could be agreeing to quivered through her.

'Immaterial,' Luisa Delmar snapped. 'I'm sorry to have to put you through this, Lindsay, but it can't be helped. Only a direct question will resolve this. Are you a virgin?'

Embarrassment flooded Lindsay's cheeks. It wouldn't have been as bad if Nick Farraday's glance hadn't been playing over her face in unbridled amusement. She wriggled in discomfort, wishing she'd never set eyes on that outrageously handsome, arrogant, smirking countenance. If only the power of thought were such that it was possible for her

34

to transport herself a million miles away.

'Do you want me to repeat the question?' Luisa Delmar inquired, uncaring of the turmoil she was causing. 'No, Madame,' Lindsay whispered.

'No, you are not a virgin?'

'No, I don't want you to repeat the question.'

'So you are a virgin?'

'Yes, Madame.'

'Why not say so in the first place? Why make such a song and dance about it? As for you, Nick, you can wipe that silly grin off your face, because it doesn't make any difference. I'm not saying that I don't believe the girl, because I do. She's painfully honest.'

'Then *what*?'

'Do I have to remind you? Woman awakening . . . a young girl in a white dress with the dawning awareness of her own power, the potency of her own appeal, shy and hesitant, hovering on the brink. Not racing toward it at a breakneck pace! Get out of here and take her with you. You're stupid. I have no more patience left.'

'Now, Luisa, the doctor said you mustn't get too excited.'

'How can I help it when the one person I've put my trust in to make the load lighter in my few remaining years turns out to be an imbecile?'

'Luisa,' he reproved gently.

35

She gave a sulky sniff. 'Go!' she said.

Lindsay had already shuffled off the bed and was on her feet, ready for flight.

'You may come again, child,' Luisa Delmar informed her in the manner of royalty granting an audience. 'In spite of everything, I find you quite charming. I am not so petty-minded that I would hold your natural feminine inclinations against you. I well remember being twenty-two myself. Sometimes the distant past is more vivid to me than the events of yesterday. You're not suitable for what we have in mind, but at another time I know I could enjoy your company. So you may come again.'

'Thank you, Madame,' Lindsay said awkwardly, hoping she would be allowed to leave quickly, yet knowing from the set of Nick Farraday's jaw that she still had a few more uncomfortable moments to suffer through.

'Lindsay is absolutely right for what we want. You'll come round to admitting it.'

'I won't,' said Luisa.

'You will, because you're a wise woman and you won't spite yourself to prove me wrong. Lindsay will come again. You two can look forward to seeing much, much more of one another. So much that you'll possibly end up being screamingly bored with each other, because I'm relying on your help to guide and groom her.'

Lindsay had almost begun to feel sorry for

36

Nick Farraday, on the receiving end of his grandmother's sharp tongue as he was. But the situation was redressed as he issued the softly spoken rebuke. If Luisa Delmar were the queen of wisdom, then Nick Farraday was the prince of guile. The admonition was wrapped in a compliment. Because you're a wise woman . . . And then he'd trotted out a plea for assistance. I'm relying on your help to guide and groom Lindsay . . .

What woman could resist such adept handling? Even Luisa Delmar wasn't impervious to it, as shown by the softening of her expression.

Nick Farraday went on to demonstrate the full capacity of his talent for subtlety and shrewdness by taking immediate advantage of the ground he had gained to deliver his parting shot. 'Just one more thing—a misconception to clear up. You have an excellent memory for both past and present events. You know that you have been intolerably rude to Lindsay both in your manner and the directness of your questions, and in your cunning you're trying to gain her sympathy. Don't do it again. Now we will go. Come!'

Luisa Delmar's throaty chuckle told Lindsay that this verbal sparring was a regular happening, one that she thoroughly enjoyed.

As she scrambled after Nick Farraday, Lindsay's most fervent wish was to avoid having to go back to the party. 'I would like to go home,' she said.

'Precisely where I'm taking you,' she was informed.

'That's not necessary. I came in a cab, and I see no reason why I shouldn't go home the same way.'

'Reason? What do women know of reason? I have enough with one impossible woman to deal with, so I'll thank you not to make life more difficult than it already is. I'm taking you home, so no more arguments, please.'

'Don't I have any say in the matter?'

'No.'

'I think you are the most arrogant, overbearing—'

'Enough! You're not even original I've heard it all before.'

He snapped his fingers, issued a curt command, and in the time it took for Lindsay's coat to be located and for them to get downstairs, a silver limousine had arrived at the entrance, the chauffeur hovering by an open door.

'I'll drive myself, thank you, Baxter,' Nick Farraday said, ushering Lindsay into the subdued luxury of the automobile before walking round the front to get in and sit beside her.

He moved into the stream of traffic without asking her where she lived. She recalled that his grandmother had asked her during that embarrassing catechism. Lindsay saw that he was heading in the right direction, and she knew that he had committed that piece of information to memory upon hearing it back at the penthouse. Because the Knightsbridge traffic was fierce and his attention didn't seem to be on his driving, she prayed that they wouldn't have an accident. She relaxed only when she realized that the man and machine were practically extensions of each other. He was so expert that a quarter of his attention was all that was required for him to come up to the average motorist's best.

'Good night, Mr. Farraday. Thank you for the lift,' she said punctiliously as he pulled up at the curb.

She sprang out with the agility of a kitten, but he was faster, and he joined her almost as soon as her feet touched the sidewalk. She tried the 'thank you' routine again at the door of the apartment block, but with little hope of success, so she wasn't surprised when he accompanied her right to her door. It had become obvious that he was a keen devotee of a health club, or whatever he did to keep fit, because her apartment was seven floors up in a building not served by an elevator, and his breathing hadn't even quickened during their ascent.

When he held out his arm she knew it was for her key and not to shake her hand goodnight. She surrendered the key, sighing with helpless frustration. But when he entered her apartment with her, she decided that he had pressed his privilege far enough.

'Now, look here, Mr. Farraday—'

'I've told you before to call me Nick,' he said, looking round with interest.

Even to her own eyes the apartment suddenly seemed very small and cramped. After his spacious, twenty-four hour camera-scanned luxury penthouse, she had to wonder what he thought of these modest living quarters. The additional bits and pieces she'd bought the pièce de resistance her big overstuffed armchair—to supplement the spartan furnishings which had come with the apartment didn't seem to compensate for the place's deficiencies when viewed from his perspective.

Nothing of his thoughts showed on his face, although his words proved most revealing. 'Mmmm, this needs some thinking out.'

'What does?'

'It will do for the moment, but you won't be able to stay here once things get moving.'

'I like it here. I'm staying put.'

'I can see you've made the best of things . . .'

'Thank you.'

'. . . but, other major considerations aside, I don't propose to climb Mount Blanc every time I come to see you.'

'This is a one-off, Mr. Farraday. You won't have cause to see me again.' She paused. 'What major considerations?' she asked curiously.

'You'll be a hot property. As such, you'll require some form of protection. But you don't have to worry your head about that now.'

'I won't have to worry my head about that ever! I'm not interested in any deal you might propose.'

She might not have spoken for all the notice he took. 'You could move into my place. There's room enough, that's for sure, and with Luisa there, no one in his right mind could deny the fact that you would be adequately chaperoned. That might sound archaic, but it's all part of the image.'

'Oh, of course!' Lindsay said with heavy sarcasm. 'And Madame Delmar will welcome me with open arms.'

'You may have a point. Luisa was rather set against the idea of using you. She can be very stubborn when she sets her mind to it.'

Like someone else I've been unfortunate enough to come to know, thought Lindsay, fuming silently.

'I'm not saying she would do anything to show her resentment at being overruled, only that perhaps in the circumstances you'd be more comfortable in an apartment of your own.'

She stared at him in wide-eyed amazement. 'I *have* an apartment. This one. Will you stop trying to organize my life!'

He didn't answer her, just stalked into her

41

bedroom, where he threw open the doors of her closet. A scathing finger trailed over the contents; then with a swipe he crushed her wardrobe into the tiniest space possible.

'What are you doing?' she gasped incredulously.

'Passing an opinion. You really do need to be taken in hand. What are your statistics?'

It was a nightmare. As well as rehousing her, was he also proposing to fit her out with a new wardrobe? His callous indifference to her own desires was maddening.

'I refuse to tell you.'

'Just as you like. It isn't vital. I was just trying to make it easier for you. This way is more pleasurable for me,' he said, his gaze lowering from the indignant lift of her chin, making a slow and detailed inspection, pausing for seemingly endless moments on her breasts and the curve of her hips as he gauged her measurements.

It would have been considerably less embarrassing for her to tell him what he wanted to know, for his visual assessment went on far too long. He didn't even have the decency to make it a simply analytical inspection, as the unmasked appreciation in his eyes made more than clear.

'Whatever is going on in your mind, forget it! I won't wear anything you select for me. I won't accept any deliveries,' she said, angry at the note of hysteria that had entered her voice.

His concentration returned briefly to her face as he awarded her a look of lazy challenge. He crossed the room to where she stood. Again the color rushed to her cheeks at the direction his eyes took.

'I'm being too hasty again, I suppose, about your wardrobe. There's plenty of time for you to come round.'

Despite the ominous sound of that statement, she drew her breath in with relief that she wasn't going to be faced with an avalanche of clothing deliveries.

'Sorry I was rough on you earlier about your dress.'

'You were *extremely* rough on me.'

'It isn't that I don't like it.'

'You could have fooled me!'

'It's just that it's the sort of dress that should be worn behind closed doors, for just one man's appreciation.'

'Yours?' To her own disgust she couldn't get the huskiness out of her voice or inject sufficient sarcasm into it.

'It's a thought. A most intriguing one. Regrettably, it's not wise to mix business with pleasure.'

'The only business here is monkey business.'

'You surely didn't take any notice of all that rubbish Luisa spouted, did you? You can't possibly think my interest in you is personal!'

'Mr. Farraday, when you look at me like this, I have trouble even breathing. So additional

43

energy thought requires is completely beyond me.' She suddenly realized how very gauche that admission was. Even though it was the truth, she couldn't imagine what had made her say it.

'You're pulling my leg,' he announced starkly.

She was glad that he hadn't believed her. Moreover, seeing the line his thoughts were taking as something to expand upon, she deliberately faked a beguiling voice. 'Why should I do that, Mr. Farraday?'

'You're a woman,' he answered succinctly.

'What sort of an answer is that?'

'Women are headstrong creatures who sometimes bite off more than they can chew. In combat, they often fail to recognize a superior adversary.'

'Even I, inferior being that I am, possess sufficient intelligence to know that you would be a most difficult man to take on.'

'I'm pleased you realize that.'

The gleam in his eye told her that she'd better drop the taunting tone. Her top teeth played with her bottom lip. Then she queried seriously, 'Do you honestly think I'm suitable to promote the product you're about to launch?'

'Would I be here if I didn't?' he countered.

That was what she was asking. She worded it another way. 'Would you pit your judgment against that of Luisa Delmar?'

'Not lightly. She's a very astute woman, but this time she's wrong.'

'You're that positive?'

'Yes.'

She was human enough to feel flattered. Feminine curiosity pushed her to ask, 'What qualities do I possess that make me qualified? What exactly is allure? You can't see it or touch it. How can you define it?'

'Not easily. It's the fragrance of woman's femininity, the essence of what every woman wants to be.'

'It's a perfume!' she said in triumph, excited despite herself. 'And you think I could help to sell it?' She shook her head in dismay. What had gotten into her that she had asked that? She bit her lip, realizing that it was confession time. She had been wrong in letting things get this far. She ought to have owned up before now. She shouldn't have allowed herself to be swept along by events, and it would serve her right if he were furious with her for wasting his time. 'I don't believe any of this is happening to me,' she said forlornly.

He mistook her dismay for awe. 'It won't be roses all the way. It will mean sacrifices on your part. There's something about you, whether you are aware of it or not, that will have to be subdued. Most regrettably, Luisa saw it.'

'Saw what?'

'It's almost as if you're two people: the

sweet alluring Lindsay who's perfect for the promotion barring that totally unsuitable dress; and the other Lindsay, the wild and wanton inner you. It could be just the chance combination of the dress and the casual, finger-tumbled style of your hair creating a false illusion. But then again it could be the inner you expressing a yearning to come out.'

Wild and wanton! Strange he'd said that. That same phrase had come to her own mind as she'd taken a last appraisal of herself in the mirror earlier.

'Why the inner me?' she contested. 'Why can't this be the real me, and the sweet and pure Lindsay a figment of your imagination, someone who doesn't exist?'

'She exists. She existed in every reaction you've had this evening. In every blush and every outraged cry.'

She looked away in vexation, unable to deny the remark.

'You said pure.' For the twelve-month period you'll be promoting Delmar products, you must be *purer* than pure,' Nick Farraday cautioned gravely, the thread of steel in his voice assuming it was all settled. 'Your wardrobe will reflect the packaging of Allure. In public you'll always wear combinations of white and gold. Men will fall under the spell of your allure; women will emulate you. They will copy the way you dress, have their hair styled as you do. Who knows, you could even set a new trend.'

'I might, if I were foolish enough to agree. I can't see myself, or any woman, for that matter, putting herself on ice for a year.'

A wry smile twisted his mouth. 'Perhaps that *would* be too much to expect. If you feel the need to indulge the . . . er . . . inner woman, discretion would be the key word. The remuneration, the luxurious lifestyle you'll lead, will more than make up for any lack you might feel.' He extracted a card from his pocket. 'Come to my office tomorrow morning and we'll discuss details. I'm not sure how busy I'll be, so phone first. All right?'

'No, it's not all right, Mr. Farraday. I've wasted too much of your time as it is; it would be unfair of me to let you go on. I'm not what I seem.'

'And what dark secret are you hiding?' he asked with deceptive lightness. His eyes moved slowly down over the revealing lines of her ill-chosen dress.

When his eyes returned to her face she forced herself to counter the taunting twinkle in their intensely blue depths with cool determination. 'I was at your suite this evening under false pretenses. I wanted to see your home, and you yourself, to be honest. You're a famous figure, and I was curious. I never expected you to look at me, let alone single me out. Why you did, I'll never know. The other five girls from the agency are at the top of their profession. All have considerable experience in commercial modeling, and three of them have had the added advantage of drama training. I have no experience in either field. I'm employed by the agency, but in a secretarial capacity.'

There! She'd managed it. She had hoped that he might see the absurdity of the situation. Finding no comfort in the grim set of his mouth, she switched her concentration to his eyes, but the glint she saw there was not humorous; rather; it was the dark taunting kind of humor that made her clench her hands until the knuckles turned white. She hoped this indication of her inner tension would go unnoticed and forced her expression to remain tranquil as she looked up at her tormentor. Why didn't he say something?

At length, a tiny quirk at one corner broke the taut line of his mouth as he mocked, 'What a horrendous crime. I wouldn't have thought a reputable agency such as Jim Bourne claims to run would resort to such deception.'

He had to be baiting her! She had already decided by the looks he'd been giving her that he had a macabre sense of humor. Her offense wasn't serious; all she had done was crash a party. But what if he objected to the idea of being duped, and this pained smile covered his inner fury?

'Does Jim Bourne know, or did you come on your own?'

Telling lies didn't come easily to her, and she had to force the words out of her mouth. 'He doesn't know. Lest he decide it was slightly dishonest, I thought it best not to tell him.'

'Decide? Is there any question that misrepresentation is dishonest?' Nick Farraday inquired mildly.

'In my view it depends on the circumstances. You were getting good value in the other five girls. I hope you won't hold it against the agency?' she said, a querying lilt in her tone.

'Why should I? As long as the goods are produced, that's all I ask.'

Why hadn't she spoken up sooner? She had known what was in his mind practically from the beginning; known, but not really believed it. It was all so improbable. In the first place, she hadn't seen any danger in going to his penthouse with the other girls, because she had thought there was no way she could compete with them. Even when he had sought her out, she hadn't truly recognized her plight, thinking it only a matter of time before he saw how unsuitable she was, and lost interest in her.

Even though she had fought to resist his domination, she couldn't say that she hadn't been intrigued by the turn of events. She had been flattered, and had found an element of joy in basking in such an important man's attention. But her brief moment of glory was fast turning into a nightmare.

She held tightly to the fact that Luisa Delmar had not been impressed, had in fact vetoed her most strongly. Surely that would be her salvation? Luisa Delmar must have retained some power, even though Nick Farraday had assumed full control of running the business.

All the same—even though she knew there was nothing to be afraid of—anxiety strained her tone as she said, 'You can't still want me!'

'Are you asking me, or telling me?'

'Well . . . I . . .'

'One thing I can't abide is someone telling me what I can or can't want. That is something that I, and I alone, can know.'

'I can't understand what you see in me.'

'Do you want me to tell you?'

'No, I . . .'

But it was too late; he had already launched into an explanation. 'You pack a lot of sex appeal in those luscious curves. And though that might be what catches the eye, it's not the feature which holds an observer's attention. You possess something indefinable, a radiance, the aura of womanly gentleness and purity. I've been looking for you for a long time, possibly longer than even I realize, because you have something I wasn't even conscious of missing until I found you. And you wonder whether I want you or not. I want you!'

It wasn't so much a statement as a declaration. She swallowed at the intensity of his tone, a flicker of something electric and sensual racing through her.

He reached out as if to touch her, then quickly thrust his hand into his trouser pocket. Was she disappointed when the impulse that had first motivated him wasn't followed through? A certain weakness attacked her legs as she realized the crazy course her thoughts had taken. He was speaking generally, not airing the romantic, notions of his own heart. It wasn't personal at all; it was strictly business. When he said he wanted her, he didn't mean that he wanted her for himself; he wanted her to sell a product. That was his only interest in her.

'I wouldn't be any good,' she said foolishly. 'I've told you that I haven't got a model's training or poise or looks.'

'If you mean you're not like the five you hand-picked for me, I agree.'

'Did you look at them? I'm surprised.'

'Because I seemed to be concentrating on you?' he inquired with deceptive gentleness.

'Yes,' she said unhappily, realizing the futility of a denial. No doubt he thought her highly conceited to think she was capable of capturing his awareness to the exclusion of everything else.

'I don't want a celluloid beauty. Even perfection, when mass-produced, can be boring.

Those models you seem to think I ought to prefer are too predictable. Mechanized dolls programmed when to smile and how to pose their inadequate bodies.'

'Inadequate?' she queried.

'Emaciated, then.'

'How can you say that? Women spend fortunes and diet frantically to achieve what you're now downplaying.'

'Not exactly downplaying,' he corrected. 'One must admire dedication of any sort. But I'm not particularly impressed by it, either. How do you manage to keep in such . . . good shape?' He paused long enough for his eyes to make another bold, all-encompassing sweep of her body.

She longed again to cover herself with her hands, but he was too ready to tease her, and she refused to act the complete ingenue. The taunting nonchalance of his glance rasped her nerve-ends. And yet she couldn't be sure that his coolness wasn't partly pretended, a cover for a possibly warmer nature. He might well be looking at her as a business asset, but could he completely divorce his business and personal interests?

He leaned his head to one side. 'Aren't you going to divulge your secret?'

'I haven't got one. I suppose I'm lucky in that my eating preferences tend toward the kind of food that nutritionists say is good for us. And I don't exercise, as such, but if a place is within walking distance, I take a bus or a cab only when time is at a premium.' As she spoke her brain was spinning dizzily in search for some way to resolve the decidedly unreal situation in which she found herself. Inspiration was a long time in coming, but then it hit her in a lightning flash. 'I might not be photogenic.'

She knew by the dumbfounded look on his face that he hadn't thought of that possibility, which to her was almost as surprising as being picked by him in the first place. Phil had always said that Nick Farraday's brain was a memory bank of useful information, uncluttered by trivial facts, giving him an extraordinary ability to consider even the most minor details of a situation. And the possibility that she wasn't photogenic could in no way be termed a minor point.

She recalled now other things she had learned from Phil. Nick Farraday had built a reputation for being imperturbable, of having that rare ability to detach himself from any situation—such a useful asset in business transactions. So it had been fanciful to imagine a personal component in his decision to employ her as one of his models.

Thoughts of Phil now filled her heart with pain. Her brother had idolized Nick Farraday, and in his own modest way had tried to pattern himself after Nick. To begin with, there was a fleeting physical resemblance between the two men. Even before meeting Nick Farraday, Lindsay had gleaned that much from Cathy, and she now saw with her own eyes that it was true. Then, too, Phil had had his hair cut in the same style as Nick Farraday's. Lindsay had got her fair looks from her father, but Phil had inherited their mother's dark color, and his hair had been almost as dark as Nick Farraday's. Phil had also followed Nick's mode of dress, though he hadn't been able to buy as expensively. Lindsay had asked once if Nick Farraday minded. Cathy had replied that it was doubtful he noticed, and if he had, wasn't copying someone supposed to be the highest form of flattery? Anyway, this idol, this supposed giant among men, had brought about her brother's death.

A strange feeling overcame her, a fear that if she tangled with this potentially dangerous man history could well repeat itself, a fear that she could be inviting her *own* destruction.

Chapter Three

'You've got to be photogenic,' Nick Farraday stated with such conviction that Lindsay had to believe him. If he said something was so, then who would dare to deny him! 'I'll set up a session tomorrow. The number on the card I gave you will get you straight through to my secretary. Call her in the morning, and she'll tell you when to report.'

'This is pointless. What's the use of going to all this trouble for nothing? Whether I'm photogenic or not is immaterial. You've got the wrong girl. I'm not interested. I like my job and my lifestyle, and I have no intention of changing either.'

'Quite apart from the ethics of the situation, I'm firmly convinced that other things will make you change your mind. I can promise you a fabulous year. The Allure girl will be seen in all the best places. You'll have beautiful clothes, luxury living, travel . . .'

'What do you mean by the ethics of the situation?' she asked suspiciously.

'I don't like being conned, and that's how I'd feel if you went on insisting that you aren't available after implying by your presence this evening that you are.'

'The goods aren't for sale, Mr. Farraday.'

'No? I send a lot of work Jim Bourne's way.'

'Exactly what are you threatening?'

'I'm threatening nothing. Just stating a fact. If you choose to make more of it . . .' His twisted smile came with an expressive lift of his hands.

'Get out!' she said.,

The flicker of surprise that pierced his eyes verged on anger. Few people dared to give Nick Farraday his marching orders. Lindsay's own surprise was thus no less than his; but hers was tinged with apprehension.

'That's not a very sociable attitude to take,' he said, looking round for the nearest seat, by chance her prized armchair, and lowering himself into it. 'I take my coffee black.'

'I must be getting absentminded. I can't remember offering you any.'

Lindsay knew that, before she had so rudely told him to go, he'd been on the point of departing. Now she had gotten his back up; the stubborn set of his jaw was an annoying indication that only he would determine when to leave, and she was left to make the best of it.

He looked too comfortable in her big, overstuffed arm-chair. It flickered across her mind that he even looked right there, a chilling image. The chair accommodated his long frame, providing adequate resting places for his square, larger-than-average hands. She hadn't bought the chair with a male occupancy in mind, at least not consciously, although she had a strong suspicion that if her subconscious had a voice it might have something different to say. But when she was brought home by a date, the chair had been a big factor in whether or not he was asked in. The picture her mind had flashed back each time had meant that not one of the stalwart hopefuls had ever been allowed through her door. So why did that chair now look hand-picked for Nick Farraday?

She stormed into the kitchen. Hating her own helplessness at not being able to evict him, she spooned coffee into the percolator and broodingly set two mugs on the table.

A sensation feathered the back of her neck. She looked round to see him standing at the kitchen door.

His regard was thoughtful. 'I don't understand.'

'That makes two of us. I don't know why you picked me.'

'At the risk of sounding repetitious, I've already explained that I'm not looking for the most beautiful woman in the world, nor the most sophisticated, but someone with a certain quality—which you *do* possess. Something rare and elusive that almost defies definition. But that's not what mystifies me. Rather, I'm puzzled by your attitude. The aversion is so thick I could cut it with the daggers your eyes keep throwing in my direction.'

Gulping with relief that he'd only noticed her aversion, she said, 'You're not harking back to that again, are you?'

'Yes. I don't like mysteries, and I'll keep at this one until it's unravelled.'

'I . . .' She looked away. 'I just don't like being hounded.'

A square finger came out to touch her chin, tilting it upward. 'Does it seem as if I'm hounding you? If I am, I wasn't aware of it. I don't like being thwarted, so perhaps what's driving me could be called hounding you. So, sorry to disbelieve you, but I've no other option. I know that you're reacting to something else entirely. I've never encountered such deep anger in anyone before, not without my doing something to earn it.'

Why didn't she tell him and watch him squirm? What exactly held her back she would never know, but a strange self-protective instinct was advising her not to. Her hand sought a lock of her hair, tugging it as if self-induced pain would atone for the lie. 'I've already told you, you're imagining things. I have no feelings about you either way. I neither like nor dislike you.'

That response didn't erase the bafflement from his face. 'It isn't as if I've made a pass at you. I've never laid a finger on you in that way.'

He was surveying her in a searching manner, his disturbingly handsome countenance etched by grim thought. She wouldn't have believed that an expression could alter a face so much. When he smiled, even if the smile was mocking, his face exuded charm. That air of faint amusement, she thought, must come in handy to screen what really was going on in his mind, an asset in both the private and business spheres of his life. It was better than the poker face so many top executives assumed, because instead of instilling wariness, it was mesmerically disarming. All this enabled Lindsay to glimpse the underlying strength of his personality. He had said he didn't like being thwarted, and this was painfully apparent. The forcefulness and dogged determination of his character were as blatant as a banner. This man, once crossed, would make a dangerous adversary. His frown caressed her with coldness. Yet even as fear coursed through her, she was overwhelmingly conscious of him in a different, more physical, sense.

'Not so much as a finger,' he said, holding his finger aloft and poising it in line with her face. Her iced blood warmed, then grew cold again as apprehension held her in its grip. It was almost a relief when the threat became reality and his finger descended on her cheek.

She might not have been as experienced as the majority of women her age, but neither was she a quivering adolescent who had never been touched. Still, no man's hand on any part of her had ever sent such sexual awareness through her body. Her skin pulsed with currents of feeling.

His finger rested for several heartstopping seconds where it had lit, then slowly, as though savoring her skin, moved down her cheek. It occurred to her that the sensitive fingertip must be absorbing some of the feeling it elicited. The sudden, ragged intake of his breath confirmed that suspicion, much to her dismay.

'So that's it! It isn't what I've done, but what I haven't done!' he blurted.

'Of course it's not that,' she said crossly, her voice half strangled by the emotion swelling in her throat.

It stunned her that his innocent touch sent more fire through her than she could ever have imagined possible. It was steam heat, earthy and primitive. Perhaps most humiliating to Lindsay was Nick Farraday's reason for touching her. It wasn't that they had finally rid themselves of the company of other people, whose presence had handcuffed his desires. Nor had he spent the evening looking at her with adoring eyes, panting for the moment when at last they were alone. This was a cold, experimental probe to find out something. Well, they had both found out something. She now knew the full extent of her vulnerability to him. And he was proceeding under the mistaken notion that he now knew the reason for her mood: he had thought she found it irritating that he hadn't tried to make a pass.

What could she do? That question was made irrelevant by the awareness of what *he* was about to do. But in the state of shock that seized her she couldn't summon the energy to deflect the hands reaching out to trap her wrists and bring her forward.

Coming alive to what was happening, she knew that she had to find means to put up a fight. She pulled hard to free her wrists, but their freedom brought neither satisfaction nor relief, because he simply shifted his arms until they circled her. She wriggled frantically to avoid contact with the muscled wall of his chest. As the gap between them started to close, the grim mouth above her twisted into a devilish grin, mocking her futile efforts.

'Well, well! So I was right about the wild and wanton inner you.' An excited gleam pierced the blue intensity of his eyes. 'This is what you want, so why are you resisting? Are you wrestling with me to add some spice?'

'Most certainly not!' she screamed at him, furious that everything she did goaded him still further.

She was fighting not only him, but the weakness attacking her limbs. She was losing ground fast. He wasn't the first man to get his arms 'round her, but he was the first who had ever made her vibrate as though charged with electricity. The feeling washing through her was frightening in its intensity. Trying to resist it was as futile as punching air. Suddenly she knew she didn't want to pull away from the tormenting closeness; she wanted to lose herself in it.

His mouth straightened again, not because he had ceased to be amused, but because a smirking, cat-lapping-cream grin did not go with what he had in mind. As his lips lowered to hers, she knew that this wasn't going to be an ordinary kiss. She knew it because nothing about this man was ordinary. His lips teased across hers, and again the electricity tingled through her, making her quiver. She was pressed so close to him that he could feel every reaction of her excited, desire-weakened body.

He wasn't holding her quite so fiercely, because it was no longer necessary. There was a sensuous lightness in the fingers trailing a delicate course down her back. She was pressed close of her own volition. This bodily rapport, she thought even in the passion of the moment, was what had been lacking in previous encounters with men. She had wondered why her relationships with men never developed into something deeper and more meaningful. She realized now that the fault had been in herself, in her lukewarm reaction to their advances. Nick Farraday was here showing her what had been missing.

As his mouth left hers a deep sigh rose from her throat, composed of a tangle of feeling which her scrambled brain couldn't immediately decipher: anger, anxiety, regret, and a sense of deep pleasure at the thought of so much untapped joy. If a kiss could do this to her, what would it be like if he made passionate love to her? The picture that flashed across her mind, showing her explicitly what was entailed in 'passionate love,' turned her knees to water. Shock flooded her eyes at the direction her thoughts had taken.

She sent him a furious glance. She hated him for doing this to her: for the tingling of her nerve-ends, for the blood scorching her cheeks at the rapid flight her imagination had taken, and for the resulting chaos churning in her head.

'I think you'd better go,' she said in a voice that shook with a million unshed tears.

'You're holding out on me about something. I'd give a day of my life, to know what.'

'I'd give a day of my life never to have met you today. I'd gift wrap it in your precious white and gold and give it to some other unsuspecting female. Except that I don't hate anyone enough to do that.'

'You're crazy. What gives with you?'

'Good night, Mr. Farraday,' she said doggedly.

She thought he wasn't going to leave. He stood glaring at her, frustration clouding the brilliance of his eyes, giving no intimation of what he intended to do. He picked up her hand. For a stunned moment she thought he was about to go through the formality of shaking it good-bye, which would have been the height of absurdity. But then his other hand came up to unroll her fingers. He trailed one of his own fingers along the center of her palm. Even as her whole body rocked at the sensuality of that action, his head lowered and he touched the spot with his lips. She shuddered with an intensity of feeling unlike any she had ever experienced.

He said something, tossing out the name of his confidential secretary, Barbara Bates, who would arrange any further dealings they had.

'Will you phone?' he inquired.

'No.'

He didn't utter another word, just left on that inconclusive note. She was as winded as if she'd been picked up and hurled forward by a hurricane. She felt that her destiny was no longer in *her* own hands, that her determination no longer counted.

For long moments after the door had closed after him she stood where she was, shivering uncontrollably, her heart gripped by a strange chill, her face and body flushed by the shock of having known herself for twenty-two years and now not knowing herself at all. This sensual awakening was the most profoundly disturbing thing she had ever known. She would have welcomed it with joy, she would have been twirling round with stars in her eyes and hugging herself in bliss, had her emotions been unlocked by any other man. How could she respond like this to Nick Farraday? Of all the men in the world, why did it have to be he? If only she could shut out the awareness he had magically opened to her and throw the key into the garbage, where it belonged. Why had she come alive for him? It was too bitterly ironic.

She turned and crossed to the sink. She

turned on the cold water and held her hand palm upward under the jet, in the forlorn hope that it was possible to wash away the burning imprint of his lips. She threw out the coffee they hadn't drunk. Instead she made herself a cup of hot chocolate. But that too went untasted and was eventually rinsed away.

She was a long time in getting to sleep. Thoughts tossed about in her mind. The Nick Farraday she had met didn't match the impression she had gotten from her brother. She had never properly analyzed it before, but in thinking about it now she realized that Phil's description had had the flavor of jealousy, particularly where it concerned Nick Farraday's easy conquests. That thought had never entered her mind before, because it had been inconceivable to think her brother could have been envious of Nick Farraday's success with women.

Phil had had the best wife a man could wish for in Cathy. A very feminine woman, Cathy was soft and gentle, with an understanding of his volatile moods and his need to breathe which had left Lindsay in awe. Knowing her brother as she did, Lindsay had been afraid that he wouldn't easily come to terms with marriage, that it might be too rigid a lifestyle for him. But Cathy had been good for him; she had provided the steadying influence which he needed without stifling him, and she had kept a constant heart and a cozy home, bliss for any man who carried the responsibility of a demanding job. Lindsay knew that her brother had felt lucky to have Cathy's love, had felt that the women who fell so readily into Nick Farraday's arms were attracted to the power of a name and vast wealth. But she now knew firsthand that this was not so. If Nick Farraday hadn't had a cent to his name it wouldn't have made any difference; women would have knocked each other out of the way for the privilege of being with him. Not that that state of affairs could ever have come about. Moreover, Nick Farraday was no gigolo. He wouldn't take anything from a woman but what the woman was willing to offer. And even if he hadn't had a cozy, well-established business to fall into—something else Phil had niggled about—he would still have made his mark in life. His drive and his vigor and his razor-sharp brain would still have taken him to the top.

*   *   *

London was wrapped in the mist of a pearly gray dawn before Lindsay managed to close her eyes. As a result she was late in getting up. Despite the need to rush, she knew she wouldn't be able to give her best if she didn't revive herself with a shower and snatch a hurried breakfast of toast and coffee.

She managed to get a cab with little

difficulty, but the traffic was so intense that it would have been quicker to jog, a thought that prompted her to ask the cabbie to stop several blocks short of the agency. She didn't exactly sprint, but her stride matched the brisk pace of the city, and on pushing open the door of her office she collapsed on her chair, winded.

She was still getting her breath back when Jim Bourne buzzed her. 'You in yet, Lindsay?'

'Just. Sorry I'm late.'

The favor she usually found in his eyes wouldn't excuse her tardiness, because he was a stickler for punctuality. Lindsay swallowed at hearing Jim say, 'It will make up for all the times that's happened at the other end of the day.'

It was true that Lindsay often stayed at her desk after closing time, but no mention had been made of this before, and she glowed at being appreciated. 'I didn't think you'd noticed.'

'I notice a lot of things I don't comment on. Come in, will you?'

'I'll be right there.'

But the step that took her into his office was less enthusiastic than her voice. Lindsay knew that Jim Bourne would want to know all about the previous night, and she wasn't looking forward to relating even the bit she could tell him.

'Won't be a minute,' Jim said, not looking up from his scribbling. She had never known anyone who could write with his speed. At the same time he waved his hand to indicate that she should sit down.

When he looked up, his eyes couldn't decide what emotion to express. She saw dry humor, annoyance, wonder and exasperation. 'Barbara Bates, Nick Farraday's secretary, has just been on the phone.'

'Oh, you know, then?' That was one hurdle over, at least.

'She said you had to report this morning for tests. Miss Bates gives very little away, but the way your presence is demanded says all.'

'I don't know why Nick Farraday picked me to promote his new product. It's utterly ridiculous. When I woke up this morning I was hoping I'd dreamed it.'

'No dream, and it could be a nightmare for me, having to replace you.'

'I told Nick Farraday that I wasn't interested, and that I wouldn't show up for the tests.'

'You *what?*'

'You don't have to bellow at me,' Lindsay said softly.

'I didn't think I'd heard right. No one in his right mind turns Nick Farraday down.'

Lindsay could have said that that was true. She *hadn't* been in her right mind since meeting Nick Farraday. Instead she said firmly, '*I* did.'

'Much good it's done you. A car is coming

for you in—' he checked his watch—'just under half an hour.'

'Do I have to go?'

She was thinking of the implied threat Nick Farraday had made, and something of this recollection altered her voice. Jim Bourne picked up on it. For the first time in their acquaintance, his earthy-brown eyes, symbolic for her of what the good earth stood for, a stability which you could trust to never let you down, did not quite meet hers. 'That guy wields a lot of power, Lindsay.'

'I know, but . . .'

'What have you got against him? And don't say nothing, or that you dislike his type on principle, because it's obvious that it's something more, something pretty deep-rooted which is going to ruin the chance of a lifetime if you're fool enough to let it. Do you know what you'd be passing up? The last time they went to town this way was to launch the Delmar Woman line.'

Delmar Woman, in its attractive aquamarine packaging, included an array of cosmetics and toiletries that could be found on almost every fashionable woman's bathroom shelf, including Lindsay's. Introduced with tremendous fanfare, the line had been an instant success, and sales had risen steadily over the years until it had eclipsed its fiercest rivals in popularity.

'The budget will run into millions of

pounds. The coverage will be worldwide. Paris would be at your feet. Rome would romanticize your name. I know you've always had a hankering to go to Hawaii, because you've told me so. Well that, and many other glamor spots you'd never have dreamed of seeing, will be within your reach.'

'You're wasting your breath, Jim. The icing on the cake doesn't seem as sweet when you consider the inedible bits that have to be swallowed to get to it,' she said with quiet determination.

'You make it hard on a guy,' he grunted. 'The fact is, I don't have the muscle to take on Farraday.'

'That doesn't sound like you, Jim.'

'No, it doesn't.' His forehead furrowed in thought as he considered that truth. If she knew the man at all, he was searching for a way out that wouldn't bruise his ego. 'I enjoy a contest and normally, no matter what, I'd be in there fighting if I thought I'd have a ghost of a chance. But this time, even if the odds were more even, it wouldn't make a bit of difference; I'd still take a back seat. I couldn't live with my conscience if I thought I was in any way responsible for making you miss a golden opportunity. Anyway, what inedible bits?'

Irrespective of whether or not she wanted to tell him, she knew she had to. On top of that, she wanted to spill out all the invective and bitterness bottled up in her. Then, perhaps, Jim Bourne would be able to get her out of this predicament.

As she opened her mouth to begin speaking, it occurred to her that while Jim had been talking his left hand had lowered beneath the level of his desk. But she didn't think anything of it. Before she managed to utter more than two or three words, however, Denise, another girl in his employ, burst in carrying a bulging file.

'I hope you realize you've got an appointment with . . .' With impeccable timing Denise's eyes widened at the sight of Lindsay. 'Oh, I thought you were alone. I'm sorry to intrude. Perhaps I should . . .'

'No, it's all right, Denise,' Jim Bourne assured smoothly. 'You were perfectly in order to come in. I'd completely forgotten, and I've a lot of boning up to do.' Switching his attention to Lindsay, he said ruefully, 'You see how it is? Perhaps we'll get a chance to talk later. How about when you report back to tell me how the tests went?'

'Sure,' Lindsay agreed, her unwavering glance giving away none of her feelings of inner collapse.

Jim had, of course, pressed the tiny button beneath the desk, bringing Denise in on the double. It was a summons which Lindsay herself had answered on countless occasions to cut short a sticky interview that Jim Bourne wanted to end.

She knew that if she asked Denise for confirmation, it wouldn't be forthcoming. Denise was several years older than Lindsay. She'd had a rough time in her past two relationships, and she was looking for a man who would offer her something long-term. Toward this end, she had been sending Jim Bourne some pretty soft looks, leaning over his desk in a provocative way and swaying her hips as she walked away on her long and beautifully shaped legs. If Lindsay were to leave the agency there was little doubt that Denise would fill the vacancy and, with a major obstacle out of the way, double her endeavors to promote herself all the way to Jim's heart.

Lindsay had to laugh. That soft spot had the substance of a marshmallow. And Lindsay was convinced that Jim Bourne had had a soft spot for *her*. Since clashing with Nick Farraday and seeing the way she reacted to him, it had been brought home more forcibly to her that all she'd felt was a deep liking for Jim Bourne as a man, and admiration for him as an employer. But disillusionment never came without a price, and Lindsay experienced a dull ache under her breastbone. She would have staked her life on Jim's constancy, would have been prepared to swear on a stack of Bibles that he feared no one and would fight to the end if the cause was just. Perhaps she just wasn't as good a judge of character as she'd thought. She couldn't decide whether it made her feel better or worse to know that despite everything Jim still had a conscience. He hadn't dared to let Lindsay tell him what troubled her so deeply. He had preferred to put on blinkers rather than bear something that would make him uneasy.

Was she in a position to blame him for that? she thought, repining over this second loss of the rose-tinted glasses she had been prone to wear. If only she could get them back. It wasn't always good to see things too clearly, and the sad little ache in her heart told her that this was only the beginning of more such disillusionment.

The Delmar car came for her before she'd made any clear-cut decision about her plans. The fact that she couldn't go on working for Jim Bourne was the only certainty in her mind. In spite of the excuses she'd made for him, she had no respect for a man who would throw her to the lions to protect his own interests. She couldn't give her loyalty to someone she felt was possibly unworthy of it. It was a good job, well-paying, and one she enjoyed doing, and she knew that many women would have carried on at it regardless. With a wry smile she realized that her painful honesty was getting in the way once again.

Perhaps, she mused, she ought to quit London and go home to Yorkshire. But that would put too much distance between her and

Cathy. She was worried about Cathy. It was over two years now since Phil's death. It was time Cathy pulled herself together, got out, and made something of her life again.

It had been an added sadness to Lindsay that Phil had died so tragically only a week before she got here. Cathy had been waiting for her when she arrived. She was not the warm and lovable woman of Phil's letters, but a woman with a mechanical, frozen smile, despair-glazed eyes, and a heart filled with bitterness and hate. This was the Cathy whom Lindsay still knew.

Phil's demanding job had only permitted him to make rare weekend visits home. Although Cathy had accompanied him a couple of times, there hadn't been enough time for Lindsay to get to know her well. Lindsay had wondered if her brother wrote so many letters to ease his conscience, or, and possibly this was nearer the mark, simply because he liked writing letters. At first he'd written reams about Cathy, about her sweetness and warmth and gaiety, until Lindsay felt that she knew her and come to love her as Phil did. But the birth of their daughter, Stephanie, had denied Cathy her status as sole object of Phil's attention. For the last two years of his life, his dominant concern had been Stephanie's growth and antics. He had doted on his daughter. So it wasn't just for Cathy's sake that Lindsay wanted to stay. She wanted to be on hand to see her niece grow up, as Phil no doubt would have wished.

* * *

Jim Bourne's defection had weakened Lindsay's resolve. She needed to sit back and gather her resources in order to do battle. She was doing just that, she told herself, as she entered the sumptuous, air-conditioned luxury of the chauffeur-driven car that had been sent for her. For the time being it was easier to pretend that she would go along with Nick; she would do the tests. Perhaps she wouldn't be any good and would be dismissed without much ado. How she hoped that would be so.

She was taken to a studio and handed over to a fashion expert, who put her in a simple white dress that was virginal in its purity, but which in no way disguised her womanly allure. Then a makeup girl took over and set to work with amazing skill and dexterity. When she'd finished she gave Lindsay a hand-mirror. Lindsay hardly recognized the face that stared back at her.

The cameraman had ginger-colored hair, light blue eyes, and a freckled, friendly face. His smile was infectious, tempting her own lips as he came forward to greet her. He walked with a limp.

'Hi! Bob Sheldon here. Sure glad to meet you.'

The man himself was unfamiliar to her, but the name was not. At Jim's request, she'd contacted him herself for photographic sessions, and her models unfailingly gave him a good report. One of them, Ami, was more than a little sweet on him, and now Lindsay knew why.

'Lindsay Cooper. The pleasure is mutual.' She meant that; she liked him on sight, even though she wished they'd met in different circumstances.

'Lindsay Cooper.' He repeated her name, musing over it. 'Of the Bourne Agency?'

'Yes.'

'We've spoken on the telephone.'

'That's right.'

'Correct me if I'm wrong, but I thought you were solely on the administrative side.'

'I am.'

'Lucky break?'

'No. I'm here because of a man who won't admit that he's wrong.' She gave a sketchy explanation of the circumstances. 'It's utterly ridiculous, my being here. I've never heard anything like it before.'

'No? Well, I have. Some of the greatest models in the business have been discovered by accident. Cross your fingers and hope you can come across as well. Not that I've any doubt; you seem to be a natural.'

'Would it surprise you to know that I don't want to come across well? I intend to freeze before the camera. I can't get through to Mr. Farraday, so I want him to see for himself what a mistake he's made.'

'Are you on the level? Don't you realize what a wonderful chance this is for you?'

'So everyone keeps telling me. I don't want it. I happen to be content with my lot.'

'Really? Chin up, honey, and look to your left.' Lindsay obeyed automatically and blinked at the bright flash as the camera clicked. 'Haven't you ever thought you might be missing out on something? I know some people are perfectly happy to plod along the same old road. At least, they say they're happy, and in some cases they even manage to fool themselves. But in reality they haven't the guts to accept life's challenges.'

'It's not like that at all. I've got plenty of spunk. And I'm not afraid to accept a challenge. Perhaps, in other circumstances, I might have been intrigued by the idea of changing course. But I don't like the way I'm being swept along. I like to feel in charge of my own destiny.'

'Do you think that's possible?' Bob Sheldon asked, clicking away as he spoke. 'Turn your head a bit to the left, will you? That's great. Hold it. Now throw your shoulders the other way. That's fine. Relax for a moment.'

'I make my own decisions,' Lindsay said stolidly, rubbing the back of her neck.

'Even if they're the wrong ones?'

'I bet you wouldn't let anybody, not even Nick Farraday, push you around,' Lindsay said, picking up the conversation some time later, after a session of being told to sit, stand, walk, run up a short flight of stairs, look forward, look up, look down, smile, frown, etcetera.

'Don't bet your shirt on that; you'd lose it. I've been pushed around in my time, kicked down . . . and been glad to be picked up and have someone tell me what to do. If it hadn't been for . . .'

'Yes?'

He was absently running his hand down his left leg, the one that caused his limp. When he wasn't smiling his boyish appeal disappeared, and the fine lines of suffering etched round his eyes and mouth came into greater prominence. 'You're not hiding the fact that you aren't exactly wild about Nick Farraday.'

'That's perfectly true,' Lindsay retorted coolly.

'Well, you just happen to be looking at the number one member of his fan club.'

'He collects fans easily,' Lindsay said scathingly.

'You reckon so? Maybe some he does. This one he collected at considerable personal danger. Sometime, if I'm ever in the mood, I might, just might, tell you all about it.'

Lindsay felt that she had been put through a grinder, mentally as well as physically. She hadn't liked meeting with Bob Sheldon's disapproval, and she wished she'd kept her thoughts to herself. What was this strange power that Nick Farraday had over people that even someone as seemingly sensible as Bob Sheldon seemed to regard him as a god? Well, she wouldn't be taken in. She was aware that Nick Farraday was casting his powerful spell over her, but she would fight it. If Phil were still alive Bob Sheldon would have to take the number two place in the Nick Farraday fan club, because no one had adored him more slavishly than Phil had. She knew what had become of her brother when he realized his idol had feet of clay.

She doubted that the paces she had been put through were much more arduous than her own exacting job, but it was a kind of work she wasn't used to, and she felt drained and exhausted. Her face felt as if it were permanently fixed in a grotesque parody of a smile, and there wasn't a part of her body that didn't ache after the unnatural poses she had had to maintain. Her legs felt stretched; her thighs and ankles rebelled at the unaccustomed things that had been asked of them.

Having changed into her own clothes, she emerged from the building and walked wearily toward the car which had brought her there and had dutifully returned to take her home. Her coach hadn't turned into a pumpkin, she thought, feeling a bit like Cinderella after the clock had struck midnight.

To her acute consternation it wasn't Baxter, the man who had chauffeured her earlier, who alighted to open the door for her. Neither was it her Prince Charming.

'What are you doing here?' she asked Nick Farraday incredulously as her heart sank.

'Reward time. I thought we'd have a nice quiet meal somewhere. Later, maybe, we could take in a few night spots.'

'Count me out. All I'm good for is bed.

'I'm an amenable guy. If you won't go along with my suggestions, I'll fall in with yours.'

'I'd see you fall into the sea first, in shark-infested waters at that, before I'd let you fall into bed with me.'

He settled her in the car, walked round and slid his long frame behind the steering wheel. He switched on the ignition, but before pulling into the stream of traffic he cast her a long, somber look. 'Shark-infested waters? You don't mean that.'

She was intensely grateful that he didn't seem to expect a reply.

Even as she seethed at his overbearing arrogance in refusing to believe that she didn't crave his company, she felt more confused than ever. She couldn't respond like this to him. Nick Farraday might not have taken a pistol to her brother's head, and no court would ever convict him of murder; yet he was responsible for her brother's death. If Phil had never met him and idolized him to such an extent, he would be alive today.

'I won't be bullied. I have a mind of my own. No one, not even you, can take me over like this. It was weak of me to agree to that test. Even if the verdict is good, I'm not right for your project. Find someone else. I'm not interested.'

'Was it very gruelling?' he asked in mock sympathy. 'Was Bob too hard on you? He does tend to be a perfectionist.'

'No doubt he was only carrying out your instructions,' she interposed sourly.

'You'll feel better after you've had a pleasant meal and a chance to unwind.'

'No,' Lindsay said, wishing with all her heart that her voice carried more conviction.

How could she convince this powerful, domineering man that she wasn't interested in him? The answer suddenly came to her with a clarity she could have done without. Oh for those rose-colored glasses! Before she could convince him of her lack of interest, she had to convince herself.

Chapter Four

No way was Nick Farraday going to be kept at the door. Resignedly, Lindsay handed over her key and accepted the fact that he was coming in with her. At the same time she fumed at the way he assumed authority.

'Take a shower. I'll make some coffee. That should perk you up.'

Lindsay hoped she looked calm and unworried as she nodded in agreement, thinking it better to do that than resist and then have to give in and do as he instructed. She was finding out the impossibility of saying no to a man who didn't know the meaning of the word.

It wasn't until she was standing naked in the shower that she considered the fact that her bathroom door didn't have a lock, and with that came the realization of the vulnerability of her position. She realized it, but felt no quiver of alarm at the possibility of an unwelcome intruder. She knew with absolute conviction that he wouldn't suddenly burst in on her; that wasn't his style. She felt oddly and disarmingly safe with the confounded man. But a frown came over her face as she wondered why. She couldn't come up with an answer—not one that suited her, at least.

He was still puttering about in the kitchen when she quietly left the bathroom, feeling like a mummy in the huge towel she had wound round herself. She slid into her bedroom. What could she wear? Definitely not the black dress which he had said should be worn behind closed doors for just one man's appreciation. She didn't want to give him those kinds of ideas. Once again she deplored the fact that her wardrobe was geared more to her working life than social occasions. The yellow dress would have to do.

It did very well, she decided a short time later. The silky material followed her soft curves, fitting closely on her hips and fanning out in a sunburst of soft pleats as she walked. The color deepened the tawny gold of her eyes and particularly accentuated the silky paleness of her hair. She left the narrow thread of ribbon that usually contained it on her dressing table; her hair floated round her shoulders like moonlight.

Nick Farraday looked up as she walked into the kitchen. 'Your shelves were in a dreadful muddle. Don't know how you manage to find anything. I've rearranged things.'

'You had no business to. It was my muddle, and I liked it,' she snapped. She assured herself firmly that she was piqued because of his high-handedness and not because he had made no comment on her appearance.

He handed her a mug of coffee. 'Drink this, and then we'll be on our way.'

Suppressing the desire to throw it in his face, she took a sip.

'To your taste?'

It was the best coffee she had ever tasted. 'It'll do,' she said indifferently.

'I'm sorry,' he said.

'Don't apologize. Good coffee-making is
83

an art.'

'At which I excel. I was apologizing for not saying how gorgeous you look.'

The compliment she had wanted brought an unwelcome flush to her cheeks. Or was it the assessing look that had accompanied it?

'I can't for the life of me fathom why Luisa can't see it. It's all there. Everything another woman would envy and a man would want.'

'Stop it. You're making me blush.'

'I noticed. Shall we make tracks?'

'Do I have a choice?'

'Now that you mention it . . . no.'

It was a bitter truth, but her sarcasm had failed abysmally to put him in his place; on the contrary, he seemed to thrive on it. As she picked up her coat and purse there was a defiant gleam in her eyes. She didn't know how she was going to get the better of him, but she was determined to think of something.

The only sound as they made their way downstairs was the clatter of feet. Lindsay wasn't sulking, although her uncharacteristic silence might have been so interpreted. It was just that she felt incapable of thinking up the kind of bright, casual remark that would get conversation going. Nick Farraday might have made some attempt at social banter, but he seemed to be momentarily lost in some thoughts of his own. One heavy eyebrow was lifted in slight perplexity, as if something about the overall situation gave him cause for resentment. Perhaps he was reflecting on Luisa's obdurate attitude where Lindsay was concerned, and wondering how to turn the tables and get her to agree with him.

As they entered the restaurant, the maître d' rushed forward to greet Nick Farraday. He was too well-trained to speculate openly about the new woman by his side, but he could not resist one covert glance at Lindsay as he said, '*Monsieur* Farraday. It is always a pleasure to see you. Your usual table, sir?'

'Hello, Gilbert. Yes, please. This is Miss Cooper.'

'*Bonjour,* mademoiselle. I am charmed to meet you,' the maître d' said, making a slight bow in Lindsay's direction before leading them proudly toward a table that commanded the best view of the city scenes outside.

Lindsay reveled in being made to feel special. The enchantment of it put a sparkle in her eyes and made her almost lose her animosity toward the man sitting opposite her.

She felt strange . . . hypnotized. Heads had turned as they walked in, and being by Nick Farraday's side had given her an indescribable feeling. Intrigued curiosity and tingles of envy had reached her from all sides. Not so surprising, really. Any woman lucky enough to be out with a man as dynamic-looking as Nick Farraday had to expect that. But it wasn't just his looks; his wealth and social status would have made him attractive in some eyes even if he hadn't been handsome. But then again, neither was it just his wealth and social status. No matter what kind of background he'd come from, it was obvious that no goal would have been too high for him to achieve; one word that simply didn't describe him was average. His personality alone set him high above his fellow man. Lindsay knew all about that personality; it swept her along as though she were as weightless as a feather. But even that wasn't the major thing on her mind at the moment. No, the most surprising thing of all was the way she seemed to have lost her levelheadedness. She was enjoying all this immensely!

Having found his tongue again, Nick Farraday set about demonstrating that he knew how to be a charming, solicitous, and most attentive host. Lindsay tasted French cuisine at its best, partly because of the expert way he guided her through the long and complicated menu. She felt completely pandered to, not to mention a little light-headed because of the amount of wine she had consumed. She had kept forgetting to put her hand over her glass when Nick reached for the bottle; it was much too delicious for her to refuse any. She soon felt very relaxed and comfortable.

'Mr. Farraday,' she began, a note of query in her voice.

'Nick,' he said.

'Nick,' she repeated after him, not objecting to the companionable sound of it, which matched her lightening mood. 'Say your destiny hadn't been set out for you, say you hadn't had a business handed down to you on a silver tray. What would you have chosen to do?'

'Oh . . . er . . . let me see.' Was it her imagination, or was he holding back laughter? 'First I would have lied about my age and ducked school to run away to sea. That would have given me a taste for globe-trotting and also taught me the error of my ways. The school of life is all very praiseworthy if it's experienced in conjunction with a sound education. Then it would have been back to the book-learning, followed by a spell of journalism school to set me on the way to my goal as a war correspondent. That's what I would have done, given the chance. What about you?'

'Me?'

'Was secretarial work always your goal?'

'No. When I was a little girl I dreamed of being a dancer. My parents took me to see *Swan Lake* and I was utterly captivated by it. I didn't just watch Odette; I danced every step with her. And when Odile bewitched Siegfried, I was inconsolable. I sobbed as though my heart would break. And when Siegfried and Odette were united again, it was like being reborn. Everybody clapped. The applause almost lifted the roof off. And I resolved that not only would I play Odette on stage, I would be the greatest ballerina of all time.'

'What happened? Weren't you any good at ballet school?'

'Nothing happened. I never went to ballet school. I was too young to know you had to work for something you wanted. I thought if you wished hard enough it just happened.'

'And didn't you have an understanding parent to put you right?'

'No, for the simple reason that I never told anyone of my dream. It was my very own secret, too special to disclose even to my mother. It's laughable now. If I'd just said something to her she would have enrolled me in a dancing class. She was always supportive, and I know she would have encouraged me. Not that the outcome would have been any different; I don't suppose I would have been any good. It's a funny thing, but I've kept this to myself all these years. You're the first person I've ever told.'

'I'm honored. Where do you hail from, Lindsay? It's obvious that you're not a southerner. At least, I don't think you are.'

'You're right, of course. I was born in Yorkshire, and that's where I lived until I followed . . .' She almost slipped up and said, followed my brother Phil to London, stopping herself just in time to amend it to, 'the example of lots of restless small-town girls and came to seek my fortune in the big city.'

'What small town?'

'Haworth.'

'Ah—Brontë country.'

'Yes. Not that you'd need confirmation of that.'

'No,' he agreed. 'Although, surprisingly, I've never been there.'

'Haven't you?' she said in amazement. 'Shame on you! People come from all over the world to see Haworth.'

'I'm duly repentant. One day I must rectify my error. Tell me about your parents. Do they still live in Haworth?'

'Yes. They've never felt any wanderlust, and I reckon they'll live out their days there. What can I say about them?' she puzzled. 'They're just a nice, ordinary couple. My father is most comfortable when he's wearing a deplorable old tweed jacket that Mother has been threatening to give to a jumble sale for as long as I can remember. He's a car mechanic. He used to be chief maintenance man at one of the mills until it closed down and he had to look for something else. He was always mad about cars—tinkering with them was his favorite hobby—so it was a natural choice. I think he could have been anything he wanted to be, but he never aimed very high. He's more talented than he is ambitious. And Mother is very dear and gentle. She has dark brown hair that is naturally curly, and beautiful brown

89

eyes. She makes marvelous pastry, and absolutely dotes on my father. He's equally besotted with her, so it's a nice arrangement.'

'It sounds so.' Did she detect just the faintest trace of envy in his voice? 'Do you miss them?'

'Of course.'

'And Haworth . . . do you miss that, too?'

'There's so much to make up for it here, but I often have little bouts with nostalgia.'

'Describe Haworth to me.'

'Well, it's built on the edge of a bleak open moorland. Dun-gray, thundercloud-colored moors rising and falling endlessly to the horizon, here and there the odd cottage. Haworth itself is an ordinary graystone-and-slate village with a steep cobbled main street. It's not at all spectacular, but there's something magic in the fact that you can purchase a copy of Emily Brontë's *Wuthering Heights* at the same shop where her brother Branwell used to buy his opium. But of course it's the Brontë parsonage which is the draw. It's often said that it's dark and gloomy, but I never see it that way. The house is soft with light. It's a moving experience to walk along the same stone-flagged passage they did. Looking at the collection of relics is like taking a peep into their lives. Charlotte's bonnet and shawl, her boots and dress. Emily's mug. Aunt Branwell's teapot. And the children's tiny handwriting in the miniature books, their first

90

efforts at storytelling. But it's the intangible things that always get to me—the feeling that those gifted, isolated children whose minds ran so free, weaving such fantasies, are still there. Sometimes, as the wind creaks the old wood, it's as if you hear their somber laughter. You feel that if you reach out and touch Aunt Branwell's teapot it will still be warm from the last brew. At least, that's how it strikes me. Does that sound silly to you?'

'Not from a romantic such as yourself.'

A gentle sigh rose from her throat. 'It's true that Haworth, immortalized as it has been by the Brontës, has a strange charm for the imagination. Especially the graveyard on a drizzly November day at twilight. But enough of that.'

'Why? I'm enjoying it.'

'I'm not sure that you aren't laughing at me.'

'That would be most ungallant of me after being so delightfully entertained.'

'You *are* laughing at me.'

'No; truly I'm not. I just feel relaxed and comfortable. Even with the ghosts. Seems a pity to move, but there's still a lot of ground to cover. So, if you're ready . . . ?'

The evening passed in an euphoric whirl as Nick Farraday shuttled her from one place to another. The small hours found him leading her onto the small, intimate dance floor of a select club. She had managed to avoid dancing with him until now, but she'd finally run out of excuses—and determination. She threw herself into the lively beat, moving freely to rid herself of the tension that was beginning to creep back as she tried to make sense of her feelings.

She could have liked Nick Farraday very much—if she hadn't disliked him so intensely. What had he said at their first meeting, that hate on someone else's behalf was the worst kind? And then he'd said something about all the circumstances rarely being disclosed. She suddenly felt out of step. With so many people thinking good of Nick Farraday, could he be as bad as she thought?

The beat had changed. The tempo was now slow, dreamy. Lindsay knew that she ought to walk off the floor. In the subdued lighting she was still aware of Nick's eyes on her face, the puzzled quirk of his brow, the sulky grimness of his mouth. He was used to people liking him unconditionally, or at least fawning over him and putting up a pretense of favorable interest. Yet she wouldn't have said that Bob Sheldon was the sort to cozy up to someone simply because he put business his way. What had Nick Farraday done to make Bob Sheldon willing to lay down his life for him?

Nick Farraday's arm curved round her as they danced, but propriety ended with the way he brought her close to his strong body. Panic curled in her stomach.

She raised furious eyes to his. 'You might at

least let me breathe,' she whispered.

'For a girl who had a secret dream of being a ballerina, you're not doing so well. You're as stiff as a poker. Relax . . . if you dare.'

'What's that supposed to mean?'

'You might find that you like being held close.'

Might? She did! Since meeting Nick Farraday she had discovered a lot of unpalatable truths. The latest one, that dislike didn't necessarily prohibit sexual response, was particularly unacceptable. The infuriating man was right. She was afraid to let go. It was like going off a precipice: once you were over the edge, you couldn't prevent a free fall.

The gentle, romantic love song she swayed to in Nick Farraday's arms didn't seem to be coming from the group on the corner dais, but straight from her own heart. The hand that held hers was crushed between their two bodies. His clenched knuckles practically scalded her through the thin material of her dress. His other hand was low on her back, the long spreading fingers wrapping her slender frame in fierce sensuality. She was acutely conscious of the expensive cologne he wore; it complemented rather than masked his own intrinsic male smell, a combination that pleased her senses. Each breath she drew increased her awareness of his masculinity. A scraping sweetness rasped through her mind, sweeping her into a depth of feeling that jolted her breath and blocked out coherent thought.

As a shiver of delight thrilled through her body, pure womanly intuition took over. Her face found a natural testing place in the curve of his neck. The hoarse, reactive murmur that came from his throat brought a smile to her mouth. It would have been dreadfully humiliating if she'd had no power to amuse him in view of what his proximity was doing to *her*. She had never before wanted that sort of power over a man. Some vague instinct was telling her now that it wasn't something to rejoice over, that it would be far wiser to view this power with alarm. But she didn't want to listen to its warning to refrain from adding fuel to a fire she couldn't handle.

The dreamy love song ended, and the strains of another began. Lindsay's melting body waited to be drawn close to his again.

'I think it's time I took you home.'

She nodded in mute agreement, thinking glumly that she ought to have been the one to call an end to their evening. Not until she was settled in his car did she wonder if she had been right in thinking he had decided to end a steamy situation. What if he thought it would be more seemly to swap a public venue for one that would afford them more privacy?

'It always surprises me that even at this hour there are so many people about,' she said, filling the car with mundane chatter in an attempt to block out the turmoil of her thoughts. She was sitting very erect, and as far away from him as possible, pretending an interest in the tall buildings disappearing into the misty-dark night sky that was just beginning to yield to a pinky-gray dawn. 'I didn't realize it was so late,' she said, slurring the words slightly on a yawn. It was late, and she was genuinely tired, but she knew that it was mainly an emotional exhaustion, and that it would take very little effort for this man to bring her vibrantly to life again.

Her own weakness where he was concerned infuriated her. As he brought the car to a stop she said sharply, 'Thank you for a lovely meal and a most pleasant time. Because of the lateness of the hour, I'm sure you'll understand that I don't want you to come up with me. So I'll say goodnight.'

She expected him to argue with her. Something had been started on the dance floor; and every moment of the way home had brought with it the deeper conviction that it was something he intended to pursue.

'There'll be other evenings.' The softly growled words emanated from a point deep in his throat.

It was just as she'd thought. 'No, there won't be, Mr. Farraday.'

'What's the matter with Nick?'

The influence of the wine hadn't worn off; otherwise, despite everything, she didn't think she would have dared speak her mind. 'Not a thing, on the face of it. He's got everything going for him. Looks; position. Don't ask me how, but he also manages to earn the slavish adoration of other males. I don't mean anything by that, because it's obvious that he's a well squared away heterosexual male. But . . .'

'Don't stop now. It's just getting interesting.'

'The fact is, I think you're just too good to be true.' She expected him to be furious with her. Surely he wasn't going to let her get away with that?

'You really have got it in for me, haven't you?'

The blandness of his tone goaded her to utter further indiscretions. 'You might be able to fool others, but not me. I can't see the halo for the horns.'

'And there I was thinking they were neatly tucked out of sight. You see me as a devil, do you? If you choose to think badly of me, that's all right by me. I don't like halos. They take too much living up to. My true colors are much more comfortable, not to mention more satisfying. They allow my satanic urges to take over.'

'Are you trying to frighten me? I'm not that easily scared.'

'The very thought! I'm merely pointing out that, in common with most people, I tend to react in much the same manner as I'm treated.'

Looking down at the hand that had reached out to trap her wrist, she was appalled at her own foolishness. She wasn't sure exactly what she had invited, yet her body stiffened in apprehension. Why had she let fly at him like that? How could she have been so stupid? She tried to pull her hand free.

'I'm sorry; that was wrong of me. I shouldn't have . . .'

'No, you shouldn't, but you did. And an apology isn't going to save you.'

She had been wrong in thinking she hadn't angered him. She felt his fury in the hand that left her wrist to hold her chin, and in the punishing way his descending mouth drove her head back. The kiss he forced on her might have been motivated by anger, but in no way could it have been called cruel. In spite of the force he brought to bear, there was something about it that was achingly tender, and if she hadn't had such a strong reason for not wanting to get involved with Nick Farraday, she would have enjoyed it.

His hand left her face to trail down her throat and encompass her breast. Something inside of her was eating away the bitterness and making her want to respond emotionally as well as physically. His gentle touch sent a warmth rushing through her; the pulsating feeling made her breast firm and stimulated the tip into a hard rosy bud that wanted more than this light touch. She tried to feel ashamed of the lack of control she had over her own body, but the emotion was too feeble and was washed away by the flood of exultant joy she felt at knowing that such pleasure could be attained.

Her will to escape was completely sapped, and Nick now took advantage of that fact. Since she wasn't making any attempt to free herself, his hand pursued the buttons on her dress. She moaned breathlessly as strong fingers teased under her bra to find the eager, thrusting tip of her breast and delighted it until the ecstasy of feeling was almost too much for her to bear. A string of husky 'no's' rose from her throat, but they were too weak to have much effect and dissolved into nothingness as she surrendered her lips to a kiss that explored her mouth, sending a shower of sparks into her soul. His hand continued to play over her breast with infinite gentleness, bringing her a deep satisfaction. Yet with it came the feeling that it was only a temporary satiation, and that it was meant to make her want more.

It was as she had known it would be: She was irrevocably lost in sensuous delight. She didn't attempt to pull herself out of the spin and was slightly bemused when she realized that the delicious caressing had stopped, that Nick was rebuttoning her dress and putting her away from him.

Suddenly reality came crashing back. 'How

dare you!' she said in a desperate struggle to maintain face. 'That was unforgivable.'

'Was it?' he queried with amused cynicism. 'Making love to you? Or stopping while one of us still had some control?'

'I wasn't that far gone.'

'Weren't you?'

'No. And it's horrible of you to suggest that I was.'

'Yes, I agree. Most ungallant. I'm sorry about saying that, but not for the other. I responded to a challenge. You would have despised me if I hadn't.' His chiding tone was threaded with exasperation. 'You're like a little girl with a bag of goodies that for some reason best known to yourself you feel you mustn't eat. You wanted me to make love to you. You goaded me to do it, and you enjoyed what I did and wouldn't have objected if I'd gone further. But something won't let you admit that. Get yourself sorted out, Lindsay. I find you very lovely and desirable. You've found your way under my skin in a way that no other woman ever has before. And I'm more than willing to participate in whatever fantasy you choose, but only on equal terms. I won't be made a scapegoat for your conscience. Now, I think you'd better go while I'm still reasonably calm about things and in a position to let you.'

'Nick,' she began.

'Old Nick,' he said, a demonic grin curving his mouth in a way that struck her as being wickedly attractive. 'Too old to play games.'

Lindsay wanted to stay and argue. Bag of goodies, indeed! She wanted to accuse him of talking a load of rubbish. But there was a protesting streak of honesty in her that told her perhaps he wasn't. And besides, telling her to go while he was able to let her was something else to mull over. Was his control ever in danger of snapping? No! He had been deliberate, saying what he had in a way that insinuated it was straining even his iron will to do so. She licked her suddenly dry lips. He had to be teasing her. But she wasn't brave enough to contest him in case he wasn't!

She swallowed the flippant remark that came to her lips, bid him a hasty goodnight, and got out while the going was good. Once outside, she moved quickly, as if the devil really were at her heels, and didn't slow down until she reached her own door.

It was a warm night, but even if that were not the case, she still would have tossed sleeplessly in her bed, bathed in perspiration. The heat she generated came from within; it was her own thwarted desire crying out in anguish. The light weight of her nightgown tormented her flesh with the memory of another touch. Under the delicate cotton material her breasts were swollen, the nipples hard and thrusting as if still held in that large embracing hand. Her mouth burned as if the hard sweet pressure of his was still upon it.

Foolishly her lips parted as if to welcome the moist sensuality of his invading tongue. She pressed her face into her pillow, not looking for a substitute, but trying to block out the intensity of feeling, reviling herself for being in such a state, for allowing her emotions to become so hopelessly embroiled with a man so unworthy. The shame in her heart was bad enough. But even worse, because it added to her degradation, was the actual physical ache of deprivation. Her flowering emotions had been nipped in the bud, and it hurt. She had cheated her own body, and in consequence it was punishing her. Nick was right in what he'd said: She had wanted him to make love to her. Not one particle of her mind or body was allowed to escape the torment. Her brain was too active, her limbs too restless, to relax. While low in her stomach . . . it was difficult to define . . . her emotions had contracted into a tight knot, lodging themselves as an aching void that wouldn't know any peace until . . .

Chapter Five

'It's good to see you, Lindsay. I was saying to myself only this morning that I could use some company, and here you are! I must have wished you here,' Cathy said, her exuberant welcome drawing Lindsay warmly into the house. Phil had described the house as small and cramped, but Cathy and four-year-old Stephanie looked lost in it.

'I should come more often. It's disgraceful of me.' In truth, Lindsay had thought that a weekly visit, with phone calls in between, was sufficient to show affectionate concern, but not so much that she would wear out her welcome.

'You're a very busy lady, and it's unfair of me to expect more. It's just that when you're not working, time hangs so heavily.'

Frowning at the querulous note in her sister-in-law's voice, Lindsay said, 'There's a remedy for that. Why don't you get a job?'

'What do I need a job for? I haven't got masses of cash to throw away like some, but I have enough to make ends meet.'

'I mean for personal fulfillment.'

'Oh, of course.' A sly little grin came to Cathy's lips as she played her trump card. 'Don't you think I'd love to go out to work, meet people, be in the midst of things again? But there's Stephanie to consider; she's so little. If Phil were alive, it would be different. It's not true what they say. Children don't forget quickly; at least, Stephanie doesn't. It's two years now, and she still misses her father. If I farmed her out on someone so that I could get a job, what would that do to her? Poor little thing, she's insecure enough as it is.'

Lindsay didn't altogether agree with Cathy on this issue. She privately thought that Stephanie wasn't as sensitive as Cathy believed. Perhaps she did miss having a father. But all Phil was to Stephanie was a photograph in a silver frame; she had been two when he died. What could a child that age remember?

Since Phil's death, Cathy had sunk into herself, brushing off the friends she and Phil had known. She claimed that being with them brought back too many painful memories. So why didn't she go out and make new friends? A job would provide a likely source.

Cathy and Stephanie were too wrapped up in one another, too possessive and, yes, even a little selfish. Stephanie was fast turning into a spoiled child. Lindsay knew that it wouldn't help matters any to bribe her way into the child's affection. But it was natural to want to bring her a little gift at each visit. Still, there was something unattractive about the way Stephanie snatched Lindsay's purse from her, opening it without first asking permission, to extract the candy she fully expected to be there. Once time had been pressing and the candy store had already closed when Lindsay got there, a circumstance the child received with shrieks and sobs. Instead of chastising the child, Cathy had turned on Lindsay and given her a lecture on the dangers of letting a child down. Something about it destroying faith. Whether this was true or not, Lindsay knew what was happening to a once-sweet little girl. Stephanie was an extremely pretty child, with pale golden hair that curled gracefully round her face and neck. She had plump rosy cheeks and dimples, but the corners of her mouth too often turned down if something didn't suit her. Lindsay thought that Stephanie sulked out of boredom; the child's brain needed feeding as well as her stomach. It was frustrating to know this and not be able to do much about it.

At the moment Stephanie was enthralled with a jigsaw puzzle that Lindsay had brought for her, allowing the two grown-ups to chat over their coffee and cake. But it wasn't until later, when Stephanie was tucked up in bed and safely out of earshot, that Lindsay asked, 'Do you ever see much of Greg Hammond these days?' She tried to inject the right note of casualness into her voice. She hadn't yet told Cathy about her meeting with Nick Farraday, and she was hoping this would provide her with a gentle opening.

'Not a lot.'

'I'm sorry about that. I'm also sorry if I'm speaking out of turn, but both you and Stephanie need someone. I thought Greg Hammond was taking an interest in you, and that something might come of it.'

'If you must know, he took me out for a meal about, oh, six weeks back, and we had a blazing row. He might be all right if he didn't have such an inflated opinion of his boss. I don't hold with a man who paints one man black to make another, his precious Nick Farraday, look purer than pure. Greg told a lot of lies about Phil.'

'What kind of lies?'

'I wasn't in the mood to hear him out. Phil didn't do what he said. I know it. It was all the more unjust with Phil not being here to defend himself.'

There was infinite truth in that. Sighing, Lindsay said, 'I should tell you that I've met Greg Hammond and . . . well . . . I liked him.'

'Oh? Where did you meet him?'

'At Nick Farraday's,' Lindsay said bravely.

'You *are* moving in high circles.'

'It was a working assignment. He invited six models into his home to look them over and, hopefully, select one to promote a new product he's putting on the market.'

'I see. I didn't think you played nanny to your models.'

'I don't. I went out of curiosity. I wanted to see what manner of man Phil had worked for. And then Nick Farraday had this silly notion that I would be right for the promotion.'

Lindsay kept her voice deliberately light, but she was being modest. What had seemed nonsensical at the onset was indeed beginning to look extremely probable. The test she had taken had proved favorable enough for a test commercial to be shot. The other five models had all rallied round to wish her well and tell her that she would be a fool to throw away the chance of a lifetime. She had been touched by the absence of jealousy, especially since she had been half afraid that they would want to scratch her eyes out. She had been bowled over by their genuineness in wishing her luck, had remarked about this to Ami, and then had spent ten minutes or so blushing while the other woman told her of her popularity and went on to assuage her fears that she wouldn't be any good. Lindsay's lack of experience was dismissed by Ami out of hand.

'You have a natural grace which will stand you in good stead. Nick Farraday is nobody's fool. That's what he will see. Personality that shines from within is what counts. A crash course in deportment will see you through. I'll help all I can. All of us will,' Ami had said with assurance.

How very different Cathy's reaction was. 'I hope you sent him away with a flea in his ear,' she said vengefully.

'I tried to. It's all so silly. I'm not the right person to promote Allure. It's the essence of extreme youth and innocence.'

'You're not exactly in your dotage,' Cathy observed caustically. 'Don't tell me you weren't the tiniest bit tempted!'

'I wasn't, but . . .'

'What about your job?' Cathy asked in horror. 'You couldn't leave Jim Bourne in the lurch.'

106

'I resigned last week. I'm working out my notice.' The color rising to her cheeks was indicative of her wish that she'd told Cathy the truth sooner. She hadn't wanted to upset her sister-in-law, but in not speaking out she was appearing to be underhanded and secretive. She had tried to spare Cathy, but it now looked as if she had deliberately set out to keep the news from her.

'So all that you've just been giving me is a load of garbage. You've already made up your mind to work for Nick Farraday,' Cathy spat contemptuously.

'No, I haven't. I decided that I couldn't go on working for Jim Bourne, which isn't the same thing at all. I don't know what I'm going to do yet.'

'I wouldn't have dreamed it of you. I wouldn't have suspected you of being a traitor to Phil's memory. Your own brother!'

'You've got it wrong, Cathy. I've bent over backward to dislike Nick Farraday.'

'And like all the rest, you find it hard to dislike such an important and wealthy man.'

Hurt to the quick, needled at the scoffing tone, Lindsay said in gentle reproof, 'You should know me better than that.'

'I thought I did.' The reply was accompanied by a harsh, bitter laugh. 'I'm not condemning you, not really. Good luck to you. Grab what you can in life. I wish I were more able to adopt that attitude.' Lindsay was still

107

frowning over that remark when Cathy inquired speculatively, 'Does Nick Farraday know that Phil was your brother?'

'No.'

'You omitted to tell him? How interesting! Lindsay dear, you might just be thrown out on your ear when he finds out.'

'Why should that be? Wasn't Phil the maligned party?'

'Of course!'

Feeling suddenly very uneasy, Lindsay beseeched, 'Tell me what happened. *Exactly.*'

Cathy looked sulky. 'I've told you. Do we have to go through it all again?'

'I know that Phil took Nick Farraday's new Rolls out on a joy ride, and that he did so because he was bitter about being wrongfully dismissed. And that he'd had too much to drink.'

'Phil wouldn't have taken Nick Farraday's car out in the first place if he hadn't been under the influence,' Cathy defended. 'He was drowning his sorrows, and who could blame him for that.'

'Oh, Cathy,' Lindsay despaired softly. 'It caused his death, because he got into a tough spot and crashed.'

'I'll always hold that man responsible. It should have been Nick Farraday who met his death, not Phil.'

'You're upsetting yourself, Cathy. Please don't.'

'I'm not upsetting myself. You're upsetting me by opening up old wounds.'

There was so much that Lindsay would have liked to ask. The nature of the lies Greg Hammond had told about Phil came high on that list. She wouldn't have thought that Greg Hammond was the type of person to lie; he had struck her as being straightforward and honest. But then again, a misguided truth—a warped truth when the bias was in someone else's favor—could sometimes seem as vicious as a lie.

If only she had been there to judge for herself. If only she'd moved to London sooner, She knew that Phil had set Nick Farraday on a pedestal. That had been apparent from his letters and the long talks they'd had on the rare occasions when he'd managed a visit home. She didn't think it was an exaggeration on Cathy's part when she said that Phil had admired Nick Farraday to the point of emulating him. Lindsay herself wanted to think better of Nick Farraday, so she was desperately trying to see him through clearer eyes. She didn't want to feel an unfair bias in either man's favor. But, worshipping Nick Farraday as he had, how could her brother have done anything to justify his instant dismissal?

Lindsay realized that it boiled down to a question of conscience. Irrespective of whether she could make a success of promoting Allure, she wouldn't be happy to do so while her thoughts were so burdened.

And yet the situation was no longer quite so cut-and-dried in her mind. She was seeing even Cathy in a new light. Cathy's grief at the time of Phil's death and during the subsequent period of mourning had been a sure sign of her deep devotion. The bitterness she felt toward Nick Farraday had been natural under the circumstances, but after a time it should have been allowed to fade. It was unhealthy to let the ill-feeling carry on for this length of time. If Cathy didn't do something to correct the situation, it was going to spoil not only her own life, but the lives of those near and dear to her, including Stephanie. And Phil wouldn't have wanted that. Never had Lindsay known anyone with a greater zest for life than her fun-loving brother. He had made bold decisions, and he hadn't missed a single opportunity at grabbing his happiness. He wouldn't want his memory to blight someone else's future.

If Phil were at Lindsay's side now, he would be reminding her that lost opportunities couldn't always be reclaimed and urging her to take everything that life had to offer. She knew that if she let this chance to get out of her present rut slip, it wouldn't be in honor of Phil's memory, but for Cathy's benefit. Even though she felt that Cathy was in some way wrong, the bonds of loyalty were still strong.

110

Even though she didn't fully share Cathy's attitude, she couldn't just shrug it off and selfishly follow her own course.

It wasn't a very successful visit, and it left Lindsay feeling more confused and troubled than before she had come.

In thinking about it later, she realized that in her search for an ally she need look no further than Nick's grandmother. That indomitable old lady had been opposed to the idea of Lindsay's being the Allure girl from the beginning and would surely help her get free.

She didn't know Nick's home phone number. She supposed she could phone his office and ask for it, but that in turn would raise other difficulties, because she would have to disclose her identity. Nick's private number wasn't given to all and sundry.

She supposed she could just turn up and ask to see Luisa, who had, after all, asked her to visit again. Luisa was an old lady. Was it fair to involve her? But she was involved!

Lindsay still wasn't at all sure that she was doing the right thing when, at the Delmar building, a man in uniform, whom she suspected was some kind of security official, asked her to wait a moment while he rang through for clearance.

'You can go up,' he said on his return, conducting her to the penthouse elevator. As he unlocked it and saw her inside, he inquired, 'You know the way?'

'Yes, thank you.' She hadn't really expected him to go up with her and hold her hand, had she? Goodness, what was the matter with her, then? She was scared, that was what!

Some, if not all, of her trepidation fell away at the wide smile of pleasure on Luisa Delmar's face. She greeted Lindsay warmly. 'My dear, how lovely!' Something wicked twinkled in the pale blueness of her eyes. 'I could lie and say what a delightful surprise.'

'Isn't it?'

'Delightful to see you, yes. A surprise, no. I've been expecting you. What kept you so long? Will you have tea—or coffee?'

'Whichever you prefer.'

'You must be more decisive, child. You must speak up for what you want in this world, or you won't get it.'

'You don't always get what you want when you do voice it loud and clear, either,' Lindsay said wryly, bringing a smile to Luisa Delmar's mouth. 'Tea, please,' she said very decisively.

Luisa Delmar gave the instruction to a hovering maid. The tray arrived a short time later and the girl was waved away. 'That's all, Marie. My guest will look after me. Left to myself, I end up with more in the saucer than in the cup,' she explained to Lindsay. 'No sugar, dear, and very little milk.'

Pouring the tea gave Lindsay something to do with her hands. She made sure the level of the tea in the cup was not too high for the rheumatic fingers to manage.

'Thank you,' Luisa Delmar said in accepting her cup, and Lindsay thought she was being thanked as much for her thoughtfulness as for the service performed.

There was a keenly penetrating shrewdness about the other woman's eyes, and Lindsay wondered if the older woman thought her purpose in coming was to try to talk her into accepting her as the Allure girl.

'I'm right, am I not, in thinking this isn't strictly a social call?' Luisa finally asked bluntly.

'Yes, Madame. You're still of the opinion that I'm not suitable for the Allure promotion?'

'I am.'

'Good. I was half afraid that your grandson might have made you change your mind. He has a very persuasive tongue.'

'Yes, I'll go along with that. But you're under a misconception in thinking that Nick Farraday is my grandson.'

'Isn't he?'

'Only in my heart. My only son, regretfully my only child, died without providing me with an heir. His wife became very dear to me, the daughter I never had. She had so many good qualities, but a head for business was not one of them. Neither was her judgment in choosing a replacement for my son. She was a young woman, and it was right for her to marry again.

113

I knew that. I used to repeat it over and over again to myself. But something within me couldn't accept her new husband. I blamed myself, thinking it was jealousy on my son's behalf. For my daughter-in-law's sake I took him into the business. I should have had more faith in myself, in my better judgment. The only good thing Jim Farraday ever did in his misspent life was to father Nick. Whether or not I had right on my side, I was always possessive about the boy. Not of my flesh, but as dear to me as any grandson could be. Only a daughter-in-law as good as mine would have put up with me. I felt that Nick's presence on earth was for me, to make up for all the bad things in my life. He wasn't a sitting-on-the-lap sort of child. Containing him in one spot for any length of time was like trying to hold a will-o'-the-wisp. Such a restless spirit. He ran off to sea when he was little more than a boy. I don't suppose you know that. He doesn't talk a lot about himself.'

Was it Lindsay's imagination, or did the eyes get even shrewder?

'We did talk once. I thought he was speaking conjecturally. Airing his ambitions, what he'd have done if the good things in life hadn't been set out in front of him. If running away to sea was true, was the rest as well?'

'What rest? He was many things before circumstance trapped him. He went to America for a spell; he worked on a ranch

114

until riding, roping, and cow-punching didn't supply enough action. He craved more excitement, and found it for a while as a stunt man. He fell off buildings and bridges, and out of fast-moving cars. He was clever and thorough. Everything was planned with split-second precision in that business. It was necessary for him to keep his mind clear and his body in the peak of physical condition. It required courage, too. One ill-timed move, or a body not as fit as it should have been, could have meant serious injury, or even death. When he went into journalism I thought at last he was getting more sense. I should have known better. First chance he got he went as a war correspondent, where the action was. His training as a stunt man got him out of many a tight spot, and saved more than his own life. He ran the gauntlet of an exploding minefield to save his cameraman.'

'Bob Sheldon?' Lindsay queried with a small gasp.

'Yes, that's his name. You've met him?'

'Yes, I've met him.' She remembered the way Bob Sheldon had rubbed his lame leg, remembered also his sky-high admiration of Nick Farraday and the feeling she'd had that if she went round expressing her dislike of Nick she was going to make an enemy of him. She felt slightly sick, thinking of the danger Nick had put himself in. She was glad that she hadn't known him in those days. She couldn't have stood the anguish. 'I'm amazed,' she said. 'I thought . . .'

'That Nick was born with a silver spoon in his mouth? You have a very expressive face, Lindsay. What you thought was obvious—that Nick had inherited a cushy set-up without having to put in a single day's effort.'

'I had no idea I was *that* revealing. I must guard against it. You're right, of course; that's exactly what I did think. Thanks for putting me right.'

'It's been my pleasure,' Luisa Delmar said dryly. 'Nick came into the business to right the wrong his father had done. He looked upon it as his moral obligation. And I pretended to myself that things were in better shape than they were. One never fools oneself totally, and I certainly didn't fool Nick. But he's kind, and he let me keep my pride, though I had no one to blame but myself for the mess things were in. I shouldn't have let his lazy scoundrel of a father have so much control. Nick knew that the ship would have sunk if he hadn't taken the helm. It was even more to his credit that all he had was guts and intelligence to back his appalling ignorance. He knew nothing at all about the cosmetic industry. He nosed about and asked questions and found things out as he went along. He sank every cent he had into the business to keep it from going bankrupt. He always says that he worked as hard as he did, sixteen hours a day sometimes, to protect his own investment. But I know otherwise. He did it for me. No, Lindsay Cooper, Nick is not my grandson by right of birth, but he couldn't be closer to me if he were kin. I just wanted that cleared up. I thought you should be in the picture, and now that you are, we can get down to what brought you here.'

'Suddenly, Madame, I don't know. I thought I wanted your backing. I don't mean *for* the idea, I mean against. I didn't think I wanted to be the Allure girl. But now . . .'

'I wouldn't waste my time pondering one way or the other, if I were you. Whatever you decide won't alter the outcome, so you may as well save yourself the energy. I saw the way Nick looked at you. He may not know it himself yet, although I wouldn't have thought he was that stupid, but when it comes to the crunch I don't think he'll want to wrap you in gold-and-white purity and put you out of his own reach. He'd be a fool. And don't go wide-eyed on me, young lady, and pretend you don't know what I'm talking about. I have something for you—a present. It's wrapped up and waiting for you. You see, I *did* know you'd come back.' She rang a bell and the maid reappeared. 'Marie, bring me the parcel,' she commanded. 'You know which.'

'Yes, Madame.'

'I'm intrigued,' Lindsay said as they waited. 'It sounds very mysterious. What kind of present?'

'You'll know soon enough. Ah, thank you, Marie,' she said as the maid returned. The old woman then handed the parcel over to Lindsay. 'Open it up and take it out. It won't have creased; it never did even when squashed into the tiniest space in my suitcase. There's a special resilient quality to the fabric. It's a great pity, but they don't seem to make material like that any more.'

'It sounds too special for me to accept it,' Lindsay said in some bewilderment, doing as she was bid and unfastening the string and parting the overlapping ends of paper. Even before Luisa Delmar spoke again, Lindsay recognized the gift. She had seen this exquisite creation in Nick's hands that first night. It was a dream of a dress—white, with a fine silver thread running round the softly ruffled neck and delicately patterning the wrist-length lace sleeves.

'It's special, very special. It's the dress that Nick wanted to put you in the night we met. I don't know what made him go to that particular dress. Chance, or the guiding hand of fate, perhaps. It's my memory dress; nice things always happened to me when I was wearing it. I wore it when my dear husband proposed to me. It always brought me good luck. Sometimes, in a fanciful mood, I'd wonder if it had special mystical qualities—a charm stitched into its hand-sewn seams that protected me. I hope it will protect you in the same way.'

'I thought the dress belonged to you, Madame. How can you bear to part with it? I can't take it.'

'Because it's no longer fashionable?'

'Oh, no! It *is* fashionable. It's come full circle again. Anyway, expensive garments rarely date. I'd love to have it, but I just couldn't take it away from you.'

'My dear, it's no longer possible for me to wear it. I'm too old for it, and I don't think it would fit me now anyway. I have enough memories in my head without having them clutter up my wardrobe as well. Now, I want you to go and take the dress with you. You *will* accept it, because I command it. Go quickly. Even the happy times can be sad and melancholy in retrospect. I'm displeased with you for making me reflect on the past. What's more, you've tired me out.'

'I'm sorry. Thank you for the dress,' Lindsay said, rewrapping it. 'Thank you so much. I know I'm going to love wearing it. I'm sorry for tiring you, I truly am. Does that mean you don't want me to come again?'

'One thing my long life has taught me is not to waste time wanting something that cannot possibly be. Whether either of us likes it or not, you will come again. You and I share a bond, Lindsay. And don't insult my intelligence by pretending not to know what I mean.'

'I wouldn't dare, Madame.'

'Madame is too formal. You'd better call me Luisa. I trust you won't find that too intimidating?'

'No, Mad— I mean, no, Luisa.'

'Before you go, one word of advice. Stand up to Nick. Don't let him ride roughshod over you. On your way out, tell Marie to clear the tea things.' The beringed hands crossed atop the silken lap. The heavily lidded eyes closed.

'Yes, Luisa,' Lindsay whispered as she rose and tiptoed out, cradling her precious parcel close to her heart.

Chapter Six

The telephone call from Nick's secretary, the capable and chilly-voiced Barbara Bates, asking Lindsay to stop in at her earliest convenience to sign the contract didn't come as a surprise. Nick Farraday had mentioned something about getting the paperwork drawn up to make her appointment all legal and binding, but she had pushed the thought to the back of her mind. Was it a subtle move on Nick's part, she wondered, getting his secretary to phone her? However busy he was, surely he could have spared the few minutes it would have taken to make the call himself.

Ami popped in to see Lindsay for one of her

customary chats while Lindsay was still puzzling things over in her mind. 'Don't tell me it's fallen through?' the leggy model asked, misinterpreting the reason for Lindsay's woeful expression.

Lindsay nodded toward the telephone. 'Nick Farraday's secretary has just been on. I'm supposed to go in and sign the contract.'

'But that's marvelous! You must feel terribly excited. It's not exactly every day you're given the chance to change the course of your life. What's it feel like to be on top of the world?'

'I wouldn't know,' Lindsay replied. 'I don't feel like that.'

'Then you should. What's the matter with you?'

'I don't know.'

What is the matter? Lindsay asked herself, glowering at Ami for making her analyze herself. She had an idea that she wasn't going to come out looking very good. Why wasn't she cheering from the housetops and celebrating her good fortune? How many times had she sent one of the girls on some fascinating assignment to some exotic location, and wished it were herself? The girls worked hard; modelling was no sinecure, no one knew that better than she did. But it was exciting work, and she would have been less than human not to be a little envious. She'd often wished that her job were more exciting and had some glamor attached to it, and she had traveled with the models in her thoughts.

Lindsay's frown deepened. 'What's the word, Ami, when you live life through someone else's experiences as a form of escape?'

'I don't know. You're the brain.'

'It'll come. I've got it! Vicarious. That's the word I'm searching for. I've been getting my kicks vicariously. And now that the chance of something different has been presented to me, I'm refusing to take it. Why?'

Ami shook her head, looking thoroughly mystified. But it was suddenly crystal-clear to Lindsay. It was because the man who was giving her this wonderful opportunity was Nick Farraday. The excuses that she'd invented in her mind wouldn't wash, because she knew, just as well as Nick Farraday did, that she was equal to the challenge. Was she petty-minded enough to turn him down because she didn't want to prove him right?

'Oh, *no*! If I don't do this, I've got a feeling that I'm going to regret it for the rest of my life.'

Ami didn't listen to the despondent tone, just picked up on the words.

'That's the spirit. Think positive. You're going to be a success. An astute businessman like Nick Farraday wouldn't want to sign you up if he weren't sure of that in his own mind. Come on, put your jacket on and go along and do the deed.'

'I will!' Lindsay said decisively, but she knew it was her own thoughts that goaded her into action and not Ami's enthusiasm.

Miracle of miracles, she managed to get a cab. Usually cabs whizzed straight past her, but this time she raised her hand and one materialized as if by magic. Maybe that's a good omen, Lindsay thought. A jauntiness was in her step as she entered the Delmar Building. She was suddenly sure she was doing the right thing.

Her buoyant mood deflated at the shock of seeing Nick's secretary. She had thought that Barbara Bates would be an older woman. Seeing her in the flesh, Lindsay realized that she was only in her late twenties. She had expected Barbara to have a forceful, commanding personality that gave off rays of super-efficiency. This was spot-on. But her cold tone and undoubted efficiency had somehow planted a picture in Lindsay's mind of a woman of dowdy appearance. Nothing could have been further from the truth. Barbara Bates was a creamy-skinned redhead with an attractive tip-tilted nose and a superb figure.

Lindsay sensed that Barbara Bates's opinion of her was far less flattering. There was something scathing about the icy smile on Miss Bates's lips that was reflected as well in her amazingly beautiful cool-green eyes.

She rang through to Nick Farraday. 'Miss

Cooper is here.'

Then Nick's distinctive voice said, 'I'll see her right away. Bring yourself in as well, Barbara.' Lindsay soon realized the reason for that latter command. A third party was required to witness the signatures.

Nick looked different behind the huge, leather-tooled desk. The air of authority suited him, Lindsay decided as she took the chair directly facing him. Barbara Bates remained standing for a moment; then, as she bent to witness Nick's signature, her hair brushed his cheek. He absently scrubbed the spot with his hand, but he didn't seem to find it an annoyance. His smile was wide as he handed Lindsay a copy of the contract to take with her.

It was only eleven o'clock, too early for Nick to suggest lunch, Lindsay realized, wishing she'd had the forethought, and cunning, to time her arrival better. She felt that the signing of the contract should be celebrated. Or did she mean that seeing Nick again deserved something special?

It was something of a letdown to find herself being dismissed, even though Nick managed it courteously by saying that he wouldn't detain her as he was sure she had a lot to do in winding up her commitment to Jim Bourne. How true that was.

*   *   *

Lindsay was seated at her desk, endeavoring to clear up the backlog in order to leave everything up to date for her successor, when Ami burst in on her, clutching a newspaper.

'This is a goodie,' she said spreading it open before Lindsay and stabbing a finger at the Hot Sauce gossip column. 'Or a baddie, depending on how you look at it.'

Maisie Pellman, who wrote the column, could be rated as one of the wittiest columnists in town, but she was also one to be feared, because her barbed pen was often unkind to its victims. She rarely bent the truth, even if she did occasionally pass on a slightly warped version of it, and people therefore took notice of what she wrote.

Puzzled by Ami's interest, Lindsay read:

Hot tip from Hot Sauce. Rumor has it that the House of Delmar is all set to launch its latest breathlessly awaited product. But—interesting point—has the devastating and eminently eligible Nick Farraday found himself hoist with his own petard? What is the allure of the blonde he was seen dancing heart-to-heart with quite recently, the one who is tipped as being groomed to promote the hush-hush commodity? The gleam in Nick Farraday's eye suggested he meant business. Wink-wink. Nudge-nudge.

'Nick Farraday isn't going to like this one

bit. I'm not too gone on it myself,' Lindsay declared crossly.

'I guess Nick Farraday is used to living under a microscope. But I'm with you in thinking that he isn't going to appreciate this kind of advance publicity. What is the allure? she asks. Well, I'm asking, has the word "allure" anything to do with the name of the product? Even the name itself?'

'I can't tell you that!'

'You just have, by not denying it. Makes you wonder where they get their information from,' Ami said reflectively.

'Just what I was thinking myself,' Lindsay gloomily retorted.

'I suppose there's always one person with a grudge who's spiteful enough to let something drop in the right ear.'

'Not me. I haven't breathed a word.'

'Who's accusing you? You have no ax to grind with Nick Farraday. And if he thinks this column in any way sullies the image, you've everything to lose. You would almost certainly be dropped. No, if I know Nick Farraday, he'll start digging for someone with a score to settle. I wouldn't like to be in their shoes. Don't look so worried, honey; I'm being unduly pessimistic. Don't take any notice of me. I'm sure it'll all blow over and won't spoil your big chance. Although . . . I'd say it was lucky for you that this didn't appear before you signed the contract. Sorry . . . I'm doing it again.'

Lindsay frowned. She hoped that Nick wouldn't think she had anything to do with this column. But was it possible that it might be her doing? She had sworn to Ami that she hadn't breathed a word about the promotion to anyone, but was that true? In the heat of her agitation she'd told Cathy. But had she mentioned the name of the product? If only she could remember more clearly. She had a dreadful suspicion that she *had* mentioned Allure by name. And if she had, Cathy wasn't stupid. She would know that it was still top-secret. Yet surely she couldn't be this vindictive? Yes, she could. It was all-too-plausible to think that Cathy might be the informer.

Cathy was extremely vindictive where Nick Farraday was concerned. It was a black poison that was eating her away. *Oh, Cathy, how could you?* That thought made Lindsay feel instantly ashamed of herself. How could she condemn her sister-in-law without a hearing?

It wasn't going to be pleasant, but she knew that she would have to take on Cathy. The sooner the better, she thought, lifting up the telephone receiver and dialing the number.

A few seconds later she was saying, 'Cathy, is that you? Lindsay here. I've got something to ask you. Do you remember my telling you about the new product that Nick Farraday wants me to promote for him?'

127

'Yes.'

'Did I mention the name of it, and if I did . . .'

'I've read the Hot Sauce column, and I know what you're getting at. Yes, you did, and no, I didn't. For a very good reason—I didn't think of it, else I might have.'

'Thanks for your honesty,' Lindsay said. 'I'm sorry for having to ask you.' She believed that Cathy hadn't leaked anything, if only for the reason she had just given.

Lindsay wished she'd been straight with Nick Farraday at the beginning about her relationship to Phil. She had a niggling suspicion that Ami knew what she was talking about, and that Nick would start digging to find a likely culprit to pin the leak on. It would be better if she told him that Phil was her brother rather than left him to find out for himself.

The second phone call she made was even less enjoyable than the first. As it was during working hours, the best place to catch Nick was at his office. When Lindsay got through the cool composed voice of Barbara Bates did nothing for her confidence; on the contrary, it gave her a sinking feeling. How could she think, Lindsay further pondered, that someone as busy as Nick Farraday would drop everything to speak to her?

Lindsay wondered if it was a deliberate attempt on Ms. Bates's part to undermine her confidence still more when she was allowed to listen in and hear the secretary say, 'I'm sorry to disturb you, Nick. I know it's inconvenient to break in now, but Miss Cooper is on the line. Do you want to speak to her?' Even as Lindsay fumed at the disparaging tone that implied what a nuisance this was, a click cut off Nick's reply.

She was kept waiting so long that Nick's peremptory bark came as something of a surprise. 'Well, Lindsay, what is it?'

'Could I see you, please? There's something I have to tell you.'

'Has it anything to do with the little gem dropped in the Hot Sauce gossip column?'

'Oh, you've read it as well,' Lindsay said foolishly.

'Obviously,' he drawled in an exasperated this-is-wasting-time intonation. 'Well, has it?'

'Indirectly. I'd like to see you this evening, if it's at all possible. I can come round to your suite. Or you could come to my apartment, if you prefer.'

'And wait avidly for tomorrow's column to find out what Ms. Pellman makes of that?'

'Mmmmm . . . yes. That would be indiscreet, I suppose. What do you suggest?'

'Do you know a restaurant called—' He broke off abruptly. 'To hell with it!' In her mind's eye she saw the black brows meeting in a hard frown. 'Neither Maisie Pellman nor any other inquisitive gossip-monger is going to make me resort to clandestine meetings. I'll collect you. About eight.'

He didn't wait to find out if that was all right with her, just rang off, leaving her quivering with indignation at the terse way he had ended the conversation.

Maisie Pellman's item had aroused Nick's fury. Lindsay wasn't sure, but she suspected that he intended to take her somewhere where they were sure to be seen—as an act of defiance. In his shoes, she would have done the same thing.

If she was going to be shown off, she had to be a credit to him. What on earth was she going to wear? She really had to consider doing some serious shopping, a thought that struck her as being funny. She was planning to do serious shopping for the frivolities that were missing from her wardrobe!

She did have one absolutely exquisite dress, too dressy for an ordinary occasion. But this occasion warranted it. Luisa's good-luck dress. On doing up the incredible number of tiny buttons that extended the length of the close-fitting bodice to the level of her hip bones, she realized that, irrespective of whether the charm Luisa said was sewn into the dress worked or not, she looked charming in it. The demureness of the long lacy sleeves and the gentle ruffles encircling her throat suited her. Her limbs seemed to have acquired an added fluidity, and she moved with more poise and self-assurance than usual. When she had bought the dress, Luisa must have been exactly her size, because the fit was perfect.

Lindsay didn't know whether to wait for Nick at the entrance of her apartment block or let him climb Mont Blanc, as he had jokingly called the seven flights of stairs to her door. She decided on the former, but he forestalled her by arriving fifteen minutes early.

Smoothing her hands over the luxurious texture of her dress for luck, she went to answer his knock. There wasn't the slightest doubt in her mind that the impatient rap of knuckles was his summons. At the same time she knew that she was going to have to take herself in hand; there was neither rhyme nor reason in her feeling guilty. If you felt guilty you looked guilty, Lindsay said to herself, and if she carried on like this, Nick Farraday wasn't going to believe her when she stated her innocence.

His large frame filled the doorway.

'Good evening, Nick. Won't you come in?' she invited graciously.

'As we can hardly talk here, the answer has got to be yes.'

She had been hoping the talk could be deferred until after they'd eaten, when, she hoped, he would be in a more amenable mood. 'I was only doing the social bit,' she said, turning to lead the way and giving him a sharp look over her shoulder. 'There's no need to be sarcastic.'

'You're right. I'm sorry,' he said without contrition. 'Do you want coffee, Nick? No thanks, I had a cup before setting out. So can we get straight down to the nitty-gritty? Yes, I'd like that fine, Lindsay. There . . . all the preliminaries swept out of the way for you.'

'Not quite. I haven't asked you to sit down. Sit down, please, Nick.'

For a moment she thought that he wasn't going to do as she asked, that he intended to remain standing. Telling him the truth would be bad enough without his intimidating bulk over her. Unfortunately, the confidence that Luisa's dress had given her seemed to have vanished, though that didn't stop the adrenaline from pumping madly through her system at the sight of him. His short temper and the tightness straining his features didn't detract from his sheer magnetism.

He sat down heavily, and she waited for the protesting creak of the chair's springs to subside before she began. 'I would rather climb into a tankful of rattlesnakes than say what I have to, knowing what you're going to make of it. It's a confession. Phil Cooper, who used to work for you and whom you fired, was my brother.'

'Cooper! Of course! All the time I've been beating my brains out to know what was bugging you, the connection never occurred to me. How stupid can one get! So that's it.'

'That is *not* it. It has no link with the piece in Hot Sauce.'

'You didn't have to sink to such means. If you didn't want a part in the deal, why didn't you say so?'

'I did say so, time and time again. You wouldn't listen.'

'I see now that I should have taken you seriously. I thought you were saying one thing and meaning another. It's a feminine characteristic.'

'I meant it at the time. I felt as if I was being plunged into something without being given a chance to decide whether I wanted it or not. But the leak didn't come from me. I remember your saying that if anything got out, it would allow your competitors to steal a march. I couldn't do a thing like that to you.'

'Are you telling me that you haven't harbored a single thought of revenge in that sweet head of yours?'

'No . . . that is, I might have.'

'Might have?'

'All right, I have! But it was the merest seed of a thought, which I didn't allow to germinate. It was all to do with the gold-and-white image of sweetness and purity the girl was supposed to portray. I seemed powerless to stop the tide of events, and I thought it would serve you right if I turned up at some important promotional function wearing the black dress.'

'The black dress?'

'You know the one,' she said huskily.

'Yes, I do. And let me tell you here and now that if you'd attempted such a thing, I would have been severely tempted to take it off you, and would have taken immense pleasure in doing it.'

Lindsay vowed that she had to stop getting mental pictures such as the one that now flashed across her mind of Nick disrobing her. The image was most disconcerting. She didn't see him ripping the dress from her in anger as outrageous punishment for an equally outrageous deed, but taking it off her with the slow, sensuous caressing fingers of a lover. No man had ever undressed her before, not even in her mind, and the shame of it made her lower her dusky gold lashes to her burning cheeks.

'I can understand your anger, Nick. I can understand how you feel, even if it saddens me.'

'Whom do you think I'm angry with?'

'Why . . . Maisie Pellman, for writing the item. Me, because you think I tipped her off.'

'I'm angry with myself.'

'Yourself? What for?'

'You're a smart girl. If you put your mind to it, you'll figure it out.'

Puzzled by that, she said doggedly, 'I didn't have anything to do with the information in Hot Sauce.'

He leaped out of his chair and was by her

side with amazing speed for one so big. She remembered the things Luisa Delmar had said about him and wondered at her surprise. He had been trained to move quickly.

His index finger came up to poke one flame-red cheek. 'Ummm.' To her anxious ears he didn't sound convinced. 'I'm claiming the right to reserve judgment about that. Are you ready?'

Her fine eyebrows arched in query. 'Ready?'

'I was under the impression that we were going out for a meal.' His eyes swept appreciatively over her. 'You've gone to a lot of trouble to look good. Don't tell me you've already eaten.'

'No; I anticipated being fed. I wasn't going to tell you that Phil was my brother until afterward. I've always believed that it's more difficult to be angry on a full stomach. Now that I've told you, I imagined things would have changed and that you would withdraw the invitation.'

'Why? Doesn't Phil Cooper's sister eat? I don't hold you responsible for what your brother did. I've no hard feelings against him. Regret, maybe, that his foolhardiness ultimately cost him his life, but there's no ill-will. And your confession has opened up a whole new can of beans. As well as my stomach, my curiosity needs feeding. My mind is buzzing with unanswered questions. High on the list is your resentment of me on your late brother's behalf.'

She was completely confused. Things weren't adding up. According to Cathy, Phil had been unfairly dismissed; but if that were the case, wouldn't Nick Farraday's face have shown at least some trace of guilt? Even he wasn't in such command of himself that he could remove all traces of such a powerful emotion. Not to say that his eyes weren't brimming over with emotion; the seeming intensity of it dried her mouth.

'You don't happen to have two steaks in the fridge and a bottle of wine tucked away somewhere, by any chance?' he inquired.

'Might have.' She found it difficult to unlock her gaze from his. 'You're a strange man. I expected you to be livid with me for not being straight with you.'

'I'm burning up with something, but it isn't anger. If you want it spelled out, I'm wondering how I could be dumb enough to be taken in. How everyone could be right except me.'

'Right about what?'

'You got it right in knowing you aren't the girl for the promotion. Luisa got it right for the same reason. And that barb-tongued columnist got it right. I'm annoyed with myself for not knowing my own feelings. The last laugh's on me. I've fallen under the spell of your allure. You can tear up the contract, because I don't want you to allure millions, only me. I don't want to share you; I want you all to myself. Now, lead me to those steaks. I'll cook the dinner while you go and change your dress.'

'Why should I change my dress? Don't you like it? You should. It belongs, or I should say belonged, to Luisa. It's the one you picked out for me to wear when we first met. I went to see Luisa, and she insisted on giving it to me.'

'It's very attractive, but . . .'

'You still want me to change? What into, as if I didn't know! The black dress?'

'What else? The sweet and pure Lindsay in the white dress is for the world. The Lindsay in the black dress is a wild and wanton creature for just one man's delectation—and I'm that man.'

Delectation. How delightfully wicked that sounded. She wanted to be delectable for his pleasure. Her fingers went to her throat and began dealing with the many buttons as she turned with the intention of walking into her bedroom, surprising herself at her own meekness in wanting to obey him, even as she understood why. Her emotions had been on ice for too long, ever since that glorious awakening the night when they went out on the town. Feeling as she did, she certainly wasn't going to argue. And on top of everything else, she was weak with relief that what she'd had to tell him about being Phil's sister hadn't sent him storming off in a temper.

'That's what I like,' he growled softly. 'A

submissive woman.'

It was one thing to be submissive, another for it to be gloated over. Even if his arms hadn't suddenly shot out to contain her before she had a chance to get very far, his words would have halted her step.

'Submissive?' she said, frowning.

'Mmmmm.' He snuggled her closer. 'Gives a guy a sense of power.' Large hands stroked over her midriff. He nuzzled her hair aside with his mouth and kissed the nape of her neck, the burning sweetness of it causing her to wriggle. Groaning, he turned her round to face him, his hands now encircling her hips. Held so close, she could feel his tension. His eyes burned into hers as he said rawly, 'I want you so much, I hurt.'

She could understand that, because she felt the same way. Until experiencing it herself, she had thought that this kind of feeling was something known only to the male of the species. She hadn't known it was possible for a woman to feel such heat for a man, know such longing for appeasement. His hands cradled her closer in a sensuous rocking motion that almost drove her crazy.

She buried her head against his chest in a fierce gesture. His lips brushed over her hairline, tempting her to raise her face. As his mouth lowered to cover hers in a probing, lingering kiss, his hand came up to move tantalizingly down her neck, sending tiny thrills along her collarbone and tautening her breasts in tingling expectancy. The promise was soon fulfilled. She had unfastened enough buttons for his hand to slip beneath the silky material of her dress to unclip her bra and sear her skin. The slightly abrasive touch was pleasant. Her blood pounded in her ears as his fingers traced a path to her heart, lingering for a moment to absorb the increased beat, before finding her rounded fullness. With exquisite sensitivity his index finger drew a tender circle round the tip of her breast. His thumb stroked the upper curve, then thumb and forefinger came together and she gasped at the ecstasy of a playful pinch.

Her gasp lengthened as his tongue took advantage of her softly parted lips, seeking out the intimacy of her mouth, draining her strength and sending her floating on a sea of delicious sensuality. She sagged against him, lost to everything but this sensation. She had been created for him. She was his slave. Her body had been fashioned for his desire. She wanted to give, and to get. She knew there would be pleasure for them both in acquainting her fingers with his body. But at the moment she was too weak to take an active role; all she could do was enjoy.

His mouth dragged itself from hers to the greater draw of her breast. The nipple that had responded to his touch blossomed again as his mouth took possession of the excited bud.

'I . . . thought we were going to eat.' Why had she said that? Who cared about food!

'Later.'

'Nick,' she implored. 'Please don't rush me.' What was the matter with her? To call a halt was at variance with her own desire. Yet she couldn't help herself. She felt one thing and said something else entirely.

'Why should I want to rush you and deny myself the delight of a slow and delicious possession, every second savored to the ultimate for its own sweet joy.'

'No, it's too soon.' She wanted to say, 'Don't take any notice of me. This isn't me talking.' But the words that came out of her mouth rang with mounting conviction. 'For both our sakes, it's best to wait. You've done so much with your life. It makes me feel inadequate. I know I dragged my feet at the beginning; I wasn't at all impressed with the idea of being the girl for the Allure promotion. But from the moment I signed the contract, everything changed, and it was suddenly something I wanted to do.'

'You don't have to pretend, Lindsay. I don't think any less of you for dragging your feet. I've admitted that you were right and I was wrong. My interest in you wasn't business-motivated; it was personal from the beginning. I just wouldn't admit it. Although you needn't have resorted to the means you did to drive it home to me. I would have figured it out eventually.'

'Drive it home to you? You surely don't mean that piece in Hot Sauce? I didn't tip off Maisie Pellman! You can't think it was me!'

'I'm not condemning you for it. You're a very clever girl. As things have turned out, it was a good stroke.'

'It wasn't me, I tell you.'

'All right, it wasn't you. Don't upset yourself about it.'

'Then stop humoring me and believe me.'

'I do believe you.'

'You don't. You're just saying that. I wouldn't jeopardize my big chance. I want to do the promotion, and you won't believe that, either. Not that I really blame you. I was dead set against it for a long time. But I changed my mind. And now I want to do it.'

'All right. We'll talk about it later. Now . . .'

His mouth claimed hers. This kiss was not gentle and questing; it was possessive and demanding. While he held her body compliant with one hand, the fingers of his other hand unfastened the remaining buttons on her dress, giving him greater access to what lay beneath. Both his hands went inside, moving round her back to delight her skin, squeezing and kneading and molding her flesh. She felt her mind racing; she wasn't able to maintain the fast-fading conviction that this shouldn't be allowed to happen. There were things they had to settle first.

141

'We . . . should . . . talk. Now . . .'

Did she honestly expect him to take notice of such a feeble plea? It was difficult enough to find a voice, let alone the words to speak, with his hands plunging her into a whirlpool of excited feeling, in the very center of which was a still, dull ache.

'I want you, too, Nick, but . . .'

'That's all I need to hear.'

His drugging, explosive kiss scorched the roof of her mouth and drained her will to resist. Why shouldn't she do what she really wanted and enjoy it? She went limp in his arms again and *did* enjoy it. Strong, expert fingers worked their way lower down her spine. The circular, massaging caresses achieved their aim. The favored area moved closer to him and held her in a magic vise of anticipation of what would come next. Her hands found their way round his neck as her slight frame shivered at his touch, enthralled and receptive. The excitement of his kiss, his embrace, made her pulses throb. She yielded to the terrifying yet irresistible pull that was shaping her body and making her mindless to everything but the increasing urgency racking him, a galloping fire that was consuming her in its heat. A red mist floated before her eyes. In a moment she knew that she would be lost to everything, with no way out, no other course open to her but sweet surrender. The fact that she thought it sweet was conclusive proof that she had already surrendered in her mind.

Yet the thought still persisted that she wouldn't be doing him any favors. She had to make one last stab at trying to make him see.

'Nick, you must hear me out.'

He tossed her a wry, chiding, trying-to-be-amused look. 'Not going cold on me again, are you?'

'No. I swear I'm not. If you still want me when I've said my piece, I'll go along with it.'

'Be quick about it, then. "I want your sweetness.' His hand lightly flicked her hip bone.

'I'm thinking of you as well as myself. I know you'd get a better deal by waiting. You've done so much. And I don't mean those blown-up-out-of-all-proportion press reports. Luisa told the all the things you've been.'

'She had no right to.'

'She's proud of you, Nick. And she has reason to be. You've never lived your life vicariously; you're much too vital. You've fulfilled your craving for excitement. You've kicked the dust of the world off your feet. Your experiences have made you what you are today. Well, I'm going to demand no less of life than you have.'

'Just what are you saying?'

'The contract isn't going to be torn up. I'm going through with it in the hope that I'll discover what I'm looking for in myself. It's not just talk. And it's not the encouragement

I've had from Ami and the others that's given me this sense of confidence. It's something I know from within. It's for us.'

'Like hell it is! It won't do me much good if you're somewhere on the other side of the world and I'm chained here.'

'It's just a year out of our lives. Is that so much to ask? As I am now, I haven't the experience to match you,'

His mouth rose in a smile. 'Don't let that worry you. I have enough experience for both of us.'

He wasn't taking her seriously. 'I'm sure you have,' she snapped, her angry eyes rising to confront the laughter in his.

'Lindsay, get this through your head. I have no intention of letting you get your experience from anyone but me.'

'You've got a one-track mind. I'm not talking about that kind of experience. Perhaps it's unwise of me to admit this, but I'll wait for you. The way I feel about you won't let me make love with another man. I'm not experienced enough in living. I've got a lot of stretching to do.'

'Stretch alongside me. Preferably on a bed.' He reached out to touch her cheek, playing havoc with her emotions. 'It's been very interesting,' he drawled. 'You've aired your views. Now, can we take up from where we left off?'

'No, Nick,' she choked out, jerking away

from the lazy descent of his fingers, endeavoring to still the desire welling up in her.

She clenched her fingers tightly together, digging her nails into the palms of her hands as punishment for wanting to reach out and touch him. She ached for the feel of his hands on her body; anticipatory tremors tingled through her at what she longed for. She wanted to go to bed with him and stretch herself physically. But in bed or out of it, she had no intention of being the passive partner. She had to be equal in all respects.

'I want more than just now,' she said.

'Don't knock it, Lindsay. It won't be *just* now. I don't know what fears you've got, but I wish you'd give them the boot. Trust me to make it exceptional for you. Trust me to take care of you.'

'But that's just it. I don't want you to take care of me. I want us to care together. Why are you too stubborn to understand what I'm saying? I don't want just a sizzling moment of passion with you, however stimulating and exciting it would be, and I'm not denying for a second that it wouldn't be that and much, much more. I want to keep you, Nick. And I'll have a better chance of doing that if I've proved something to myself first. Your taking care of me isn't the answer. I've got to find my own security within myself. Otherwise I'm going to be jealous of every other woman you look at.'

'I wouldn't give you cause to be jealous.'

'An insecure woman doesn't need a cause. The other day, in your office, I was jealous of your secretary.'

'You have no need to be jealous of Barbara.' He pushed his hand through his hair and then said solemnly, 'It might be as well for you to know about that relationship.'

'Relationship?' she queried.

'I put that clumsily. Not that kind of relationship. At least—' He groaned out the admission—'not on my part.'

'I had no idea I was stirring anything up,' Lindsay said coldly.

'You're not, as you'll see if you'll just listen.'

'I'm listening.'

'Thank you. Barbara is an intelligent and very attractive woman. I've used her a few times. God, that's clumsy, too! What I mean is, I've taken her with me when I've thought her presence would swing a deal my way. She's multilingual, her memory is impeccable, and I have to admit that in business dealings she's been an asset. I had no idea that she had hopes of one day being the mistress of the House of Delmar. And before you ask, she's never been my mistress. I've never had the slightest inclination toward her in that way. Anyway, we've had a talk about it. She's all straightened out, and you don't have to worry about her.'

'Perhaps not, but there'll be other Barbaras,'

Lindsay said, surprised and touched at his wanting to set the record straight. 'I imagine that your secretary is the kind of sophisticated woman you usually go out with. I must seem vastly different to you.' What on earth had made her say such a gauche thing? Lindsay asked herself.

'Is that what this is all about?' he asked incredulously, his expression lightening. 'You don't feel sophisticated enough for me!' His surprise was too clear to be anything but genuine. 'It seems that Barbara's not the only one I need to set straight about certain things. If by saying that you're not sophisticated you mean that you're not plastic, then I agree. Barbara's like the five women you selected for me for the Allure promotion. I picked you. Can't you understand yet that it's your difference that caught my eye? And you're certainly different, my love. I can't imagine anyone but you interrupting the kind of torrid moment we were having—and to talk!'

She suddenly felt as if she'd shed a weight that had been lying on her heart. Luisa was right. The dress had brought her luck. Luisa had been wearing it when her husband proposed to her, and it pleased Lindsay that history was repeating itself.

'I guess I've been stupid, Nick. But talking hasn't been time wasted. I needed to get something out of my system and have my mind set at rest. Perhaps I don't want to be the

Allure girl, after all. I don't want to put a lot of distance between us. Not that I intend to stay home all day. I'll find something. Women, as well as men, need to be mentally stimulated.'

'That's something I get in plenty from you. You've certainly proved your ability to keep me on my toes. I never know what you're going to throw at me next. I've little doubt about your ability in other directions, but you're going to give me confirmation, aren't you?'

'I most certainly am. And yet . . . it's one thing to drift into something and let it happen. But to give permission!' The lashes she'd lowered came back up. 'I'm being very silly again, and there mustn't be any more silliness between us.'

'I don't want anything between us,' he growled, hoisting her into his arms and carrying her into the bedroom. 'And soon there won't be.'

Being picked up like this and cherished close to his chest touched her romantic heart. She would have liked this moment to come after they were married, if only to keep up the illusion of the magic spell cast by the dress, but times had changed since Luisa was a girl. It was unrealistic for couples who were in love and inspired with this passionate urgency to wait. Still, it would have been, nice. Lindsay's reservations were not, however, deeply-felt; on moral questions her mind was at peace. She trusted Nick completely, and she didn't want to wait any more than he did.

He set her on her feet by the bed. She wondered if she ought to do something, but he seemed to have the situation in hand. It was nice to be cosseted, and exciting to think that soon it would be her turn to cosset him.

Her dress was already opened to the level of her hips. He slid it from her shoulders and she stepped out of it.

'When did you know, Nick?' she asked as shivery delight gripped her.

More shivers ran through her as he unfastened her bra and assisted her arms out of the straps before asking, 'Know what?'

The disrobing was momentarily halted while he planted a kiss on her bared shoulder.

'Know that you loved me,' she said huskily.

'It's not something that a man analyzes.'

'Or a woman.'

'It's something he feels. He might not know it for what it is when it happens. It didn't hit me in the face; it was a gradual awareness.'

She nodded, satisfied. 'Women are supposed to be more sensitive about these things, but I can't pinpoint the moment when I knew that I was in love with you. I love you, I love you, I love you, Nick,' she said, repeating the declaration with fierce intensity, impulsively flinging her arms round his neck and bringing herself up close. 'I'll make you a good wife,' she whispered against his skin.

'Wife!' he exploded, pushing her away. All

the humor and passion were wiped from his eyes. He was listening to her *now*!

After trying and trying, suddenly she had his whole attention.

'I thought that was what you had in mind,' she said, her dismay equaling his.

'Well, think again. I'll go along with the flowery talk if it makes you feel good, but there's a limit. The line must be drawn somewhere, and at no time have I mentioned marriage. Well, have I?'

'No.' She averted her eyes. She recalled being told that she had a very expressive face. Her pride was hammering home to her that it was better if he didn't see how she felt just now. Not until she'd managed to get hold of herself. She felt as if she'd been dunked into a tank of freezing water.

'So don't try to con me into anything.'

'I won't! I made a wrong assumption. Or maybe you did, in thinking that I'm so gone on you that I wouldn't want something a little more permanent than what you have in mind. You can't call all the shots.'

'Why can't I? It's what you're trying to do. You don't want to be just an equal, you want the upper hand. Well, I've been in control too long to hand it over without giving the matter some deep thought.'

'Then do your thinking elsewhere, because *I* think it's time you left,' she said in a hard, clipped voice.

'Don't worry, I'm going. I can't get out fast enough. I ought to have been more wary of you when I found out who you were.'

'If you mean my being Phil's sister, let me remind you that you didn't find out on your own. I told you.'

'Forestalling the obvious. You're not stupid enough to think that it would never have come to light.'

'It wasn't that calculating. I didn't think I had anything to hide. What did my brother do, for heaven's sake? What terrible crime did he commit?'

'He didn't do anything bad enough to justify what happened. Let it be. I spoke without thinking. Phil paid the highest price of all; it cost him his life, so let's not discuss it any more. I'm sorry that I got angry and let my tongue run away with me, but that's all I'm apologizing for. I've got a clear conscience about everything else.'

'You don't have to yell to get through to me. I'll believe you. Or is it yourself you're trying to convince?' she asked scathingly.

Chapter Seven

She didn't really expect Nick to get in touch with her after the way they had parted, but she still jumped every time the phone rang. And when she left her apartment each morning, and her office every evening, it was becoming a habit to glance up and down the street. Twice her heart pounded at the sight of a lurking figure, but neither time did it turn out to be Nick. It was just some anonymous guy waiting for his girl.

It had been stupid of her to let things get that steamy between them, and even more ill-advised of her to refer to marriage. That had been completely ingenuous on her part, though, and not the act of cunning that Nick obviously suspected. If she'd thought about it she wouldn't have blabbed it out in that unintelligent way. Even if the idea of marriage wasn't odious to him, he would balk at the thought of his life being managed.

To her surprise, Jim Bourne announced that he was giving her a farewell party.

'If there's anyone you want to invite, feel free.'

She knew that he meant Nick Farraday. He too had read the item in the Hot Sauce column, and he was puzzled by the melancholy that Lindsay wasn't clever enough to hide from him. He was one of the few people to notice that her smile couldn't make it to her eyes.

'I'd like to ask Cathy, if that's all right with you. I'm sure she'll be able to get a sitter for Stephanie. She doesn't socialize enough; it will be good for her. And I'd also like to invite Greg Hammond. At one time I thought something would click there. He was very supportive of Cathy at the time of my brother's death. I truly believe that she valued his friendship. But I understand they had a row. Maybe if they saw one another again . . .'

'My mother always warned me to beware of matchmakers.'

'You're not the target. Perhaps Greg Hammond's mother didn't give him the same advice.'

'Your sister-in-law is a very attractive woman. Intelligent, too. We had quite an interesting chat that time she came to the office to see you and you were out.'

'Ah, yes! I'd forgotten. Don't tell me you're interested!'

He shrugged. 'More to the point, what would Cathy find of interest in me?'

That was most illuminating. In her mind, Lindsay had matched Jim Bourne with Denise, the girl who was taking over her job.

'Mmmmm. The best of luck, Jim.' She didn't add that she thought he'd need it to get anywhere with Cathy—not because he didn't have enough going for him, but because of Cathy's attitude. 'I'd still like to invite Greg Hammond. There's something I want to ask him.'

'I'm not so dumb that I don't know what. You're curious about Phil, aren't you?'

'Wouldn't you be if it were your brother? I don't know what you know, apart from the fact that he worked for Nick Farraday, that is. He was fired on the spot for something. I've got to know what it was.'

'I only know what you know, the bare bones of the case, not the details. Don't you think you might be as well leaving it alone?'

'Perhaps, I don't know, but I do know what Phil was like. He was weak and fun-loving. I might have been a ballet dancer if I'd known in time that it wasn't something that just happened, but that, like everything else worthwhile in life, it had to be worked for. Phil never made that discovery. He went through the whole of his life without knowing that the good things were gained through personal effort. At the same time, he wasn't all bad. If he did something bad enough to warrant his instant dismissal, there must have been a good reason for it. I might be maligning Phil in my mind when it wasn't all his fault.'

'Just don't pin your hopes too high,' Jim Bourne cautioned.

*   *   *

The farewell party Jim Bourne was throwing for Lindsay was to be held in his home. Lindsay was touched by the gesture. She had felt that he was casting her off too easily. The party was indicative that that wasn't the case: that he had valued the loyal work she'd put in, and that he was letting her go without putting

154

up a fight because he didn't want to stand in her way. If it suited his purpose not to cross Nick Farraday, that was merely a bonus!

But as things were now, did Nick want her in either a business or a personal capacity? If the leak had ruined the Allure promotion she wouldn't hold him to the terms of the contract. At the moment she was just drifting along with events and pushing aside the thought that she might find herself asking Jim Bourne to rehire her.

Being guest of honor warranted the purchase of a new outfit to wear. This time she wouldn't let any well-meaning salesgirl steer her into an unwise buy. But why go to the trouble and expense of searching, she had to wonder, when the perfect dress for the occasion was hanging in her wardrobe? When Nick had stormed out it had been a long time before she could bring herself to even look at the dress. She'd scrunched it up in her hands and thrown it into a corner. It had lain there in mocking accusation until she'd picked it up, sighing at her foolishness. The only magical quality it contained was the way it so readily shed its creases. If the dress was responsible for what had happened between her and Nick, it was so only indirectly. You could never count on being in a happy mood simply because you wore yellow, or filled with melancholy when you wore gray. Neither was it true that you were virtuous in white, or wild and wanton in black. It had all been frivolous nonsense about the black dress. And yet the white dress, the one Luisa was wearing when she received her marriage proposal, had put superstition in Lindsay's mind. If Nick hadn't reached out to detain her, if he'd let her go and she'd changed into the black dress, the outcome might have been very different.

A final glance in the full-length mirror before she left her apartment satisfied Lindsay that she had made the right choice. The fitted bodice showed off her curves and small waist, while the lace at her throat and arms made her look both fragile and graceful. She had accented this look by pinning up her hair; the silky pale-gold tendrils that escaped around her face and at the nape of her neck served to heighten the effect.

When he opened the door to her and took her coat, Jim Bourne's eyes widened in appreciation. His smile washed over her, elevating enough in itself without the added, 'Wow! You're a knock-out in that dress.'

Her employer—it was strange to think that at the close of this working day he had become her ex-employer—had done her proud. The long buffet table contained an amazing range of delicacies, including caviar, and must have set him back a small fortune. Likewise the bar, also a serve-yourself affair, was stocked with every drink ingredient imaginable.

The guests all seemed to pile in at once.

Lindsay was pleased to see that Cathy had come—she had been half afraid that her sister-in-law would make some last-minute excuse not to be there. In the midst of the crush Lindsay thought that everyone who had been invited must have accepted, and more besides! She noticed that Jim Bourne had successfully annexed Cathy, and that they seemed to be involved in an intimate conversation, his hand resting lightly on Cathy's arm in a protective kind of way.

Lindsay had already spoken to Greg Hammond twice, but other guests had been present at the time, and she hadn't been able to ask him about her brother. Now she spotted him again at the other side of the room and wondered if this time she would be lucky enough to speak with him alone. She was within a few yards of him when she saw that he was talking to Nick Farraday. She stopped walking automatically, but both men had seen her. So, although her instinct was to change direction, pride made her continue straight ahead. She ought to have guessed that Jim Bourne would invite him. Unless he'd come uninvited.

Having previously said hello to Greg, she merely smiled in their direction before lifting her eyes. 'Good evening, Mr. Farraday.'

The formal greeting sounded odd even to her own ears, and caused one dark brow to rise aloofly. 'Good evening, Lindsay. You look particularly charming. What is the old-fashioned appeal of lace, I wonder?' The sarcastic slur, the gentle but noticeable emphasis on the word *old-fashioned*, made it clear what he thought of her after their last meeting.

'I don't know about that; I do know that perhaps I shouldn't have gone for a high neck and long sleeves in this crush. It's like a Turkish bath,' she said, hoping that would be adequate explanation for the tinge of pink she felt flowing into her cheeks.

'Is that what it is? And here I was thinking it was seeing you that had sent my blood pressure shooting up,' Nick came back smoothly, drawing out his handkerchief to pat a nonperspiring brow.

How could he be so cool and self-possessed, and she an emotional mess? His attitude to her in no way softened the impact he had on her. She was too wretchedly aware of the man. The physical aura that surrounded him was overpowering; her foolish body responded of its own volition. Last time they had met she had credited her body with knowing best, but her head had known best after all; she shouldn't have allowed herself to be ruled by her emotions. Knowing all this, she felt that she now ought to be able to summon up the strength of mind to overcome the weakness of the flesh, to still the trembling of her limbs and the pounding of the heart that he had rejected.

He hadn't wanted her heart and all that went with it, just her body. It was soul-destroying to know that that knowledge didn't make one scrap of difference to her; he still had the same crazy effect on her. She clenched her hands into fists, willing herself to be back in control.

Her attempts at conversation weren't as successful as she would have wished, and she was infinitely relieved when Jim Bourne butted in. Relieved, that is, until she knew his reason for doing so.

'Excuse me. May I borrow Lindsay for a moment? Little matter of the presentation.'

'You didn't tell me anything about a presentation,' Lindsay said as he led her away.

'You didn't think you wouldn't get a good-bye gift, did you?'

'It never entered my head. The party was enough. I hope you haven't been too extravagant.'

'Even if I had been, it wouldn't be more than you're worth. But actually it's a collective effort.'

'I hope I won't be expected to make a speech,' she said, filled with alarm as the horror of that struck her.

'I have an idea that it will be expected of you. But you'll do it beautifully.'

It wasn't as bad as Lindsay had anticipated. Her present was a bracelet watch. As he fastened it on her wrist, Jim Bourne quipped that it wasn't a reflection on her timekeeping.

159

Although he kept his speech short, his praise of Lindsay was high. She responded by saying that he had been a pleasure to work for and said some equally nice things about her colleagues, then stepped down to applause, after which everyone crowded round to admire her gift.

It was quite some time before she managed to get Greg Hammond on his own. Some of the guests had left by then, and the tempo of the party had slowed. Several couples, among them Cathy, partnered by Jim Bourne, were dancing to the dreamy beat of the record on the stereo.

'Greg?' Lindsay queried, tugging his arm. 'Can I get you in a quiet corner for a moment?'

His mouth curled up in a typical male reaction. 'Anytime.'

She didn't really believe that he'd put that sort of implication on her request. He was just fooling, but she went along with him and playfully slapped his hand. 'I want to talk to you. There's something I must ask you. Perhaps it would be best if we went into Jim's study. In the circumstances, I don't think he'd mind.'

'This sounds intriguing,' Greg said as he allowed himself to be led out.

Lindsay wondered if anyone had observed their departure, anyone named Nick Farraday.

Greg waited until they were both seated,

then said, 'Okay.' The soberness of his tone told her that he'd tuned into something in her expression and wasn't looking forward to this. 'What do you want to know?'

'Before I ask you anything, there's something I must tell you. I've already told Nick. Phil Cooper was my brother.'

A look of resigned forbearance came to his face. 'I thought he might have been, or at least have been related to you in some way. You had a deep grievance against Nick. I recalled that Phil's last name had also been Cooper. It was reasonable to deduce that there might be a connection.'

His deductions made it easier for Lindsay, even though she still gleaned something a bit scary in his manner. But having made it this far she had to go on. 'I want to know why Phil was fired.'

'Are you sure?'

'I wouldn't ask if I wasn't.'

'No. Silly question.'

'Please, Greg,' she urged.

'How do I start? Believe me, Lindsay, the last thing I want to do is hurt you. And Phil was my buddy.'

'I'm glad about that. It means I won't get a one-sided version.'

'That's the point I wanted to make. You know how much he admired Nick?'

'Yes, his letters were full of him. And because he thought so highly of his hero I

161

thought it was cruel of Nick to let Phil down.'

'Nick never let anyone down in his life. Hero worship does no harm; unfortunately, it didn't stop there. Phil was jealous of Nick. He found it hard to reconcile himself to the thought of one man having so much. He couldn't see that Nick had worked damned hard for his luck.'

'I know that Phil tried to pattern himself on Nick. Cathy told me that.'

'I'd love to hear Cathy's version. Or perhaps I wouldn't. She's a stupid, embittered woman who won't admit to the truth.'

Suspicious of his vehemence, wondering if he'd allowed personal feelings to creep in, she said, 'At one time I thought that you and Cathy might make a go of it. She told me you had a row. Is that why you're angry?'

'I'm not angry, just frustrated. And there was never anything like that between us. Neither of us had those sorts of feelings. I tried to befriend her because . . . if you must know, Nick thought she needed someone. I was following instructions.'

'Why didn't Nick befriend her himself?'

'He asked me to do it because I was Phil's friend, and he thought I would be able to get closer to Cathy and offer help better than he could.'

'Umph! Some friend.'

'This isn't easy for me, Lindsay.'

'I know,' she admitted grudgingly. 'Go on.'

162

'Phil didn't just aim to be like Nick.' Greg's eyes never left her face, and a curious feeling pinched Lindsay's stomach. 'Your brother passed himself off as Nick . . . to make it.'

'Make it?'

'Come on, Lindsay, you can't be that naive! How does a guy make it? With women, of course! Phil had access to Nick's cars, his private plane, his homes. Besides his apartment here in London, he has one in New York, a house in Paris, and a villa in the South of France. Phil knew Nick's travel schedule so it was easy for him to make use of them.'

'You're saying that Phil took advantage of his position and used Nick's establishments as love nests?'

'I'm sorry, Lindsay, truly I am, but that's the truth of it.'

'I don't believe you. Phil and Cathy were the perfect couple. He wouldn't have looked at another woman. And another thing, this isn't fair, because my brother isn't here to defend himself. If he were he'd tear down this pack of lies.'

'Every word I've spoken is the truth.'

'You might think so, Greg. I don't doubt your sincerity, but if things had been that way I would have had a whiff of something.'

'There was no cover-up, if that's what you're getting at, except to protect Phil's family, particularly the kid. Nick went to a lot of trouble to save her from unnecessary suffering

163

later on in life. He didn't want anything that wasn't her fault to catch up with her. You know how people like digging things up, the way their minds work. Like father, like son, or in this case, daughter.'

'What do you mean by cover-up?'

'I've said too much already. Nick will kill me if he finds out.'

'If you don't tell me, Nick won't get the chance, because I'll have done it.'

'I guess you're right. I can't stop now. So . . . Phil was getting away with it nicely. It all blew up in his face when one of his girlfriends slapped a paternity suit on Nick. At first Nick didn't take a lot of notice. He knew two things, that he was innocent, and that a man in his position is prey to that sort of thing, along with kidnap bids and the like. There's always someone on the look-out for a way to make a fast buck. The suit was handed to his lawyer to be dealt with in the usual way. Routine, inquiries turned up the fact that the man in question wasn't Nick, but Phil.'

'No! This is preposterous. Stephanie is the only child Phil has fathered.'

'I don't know about that. Nick fought this particular case, and it was proved that Phil couldn't possibly be the father, so the suit was dropped. As I said just now, hush money was paid to keep it under cover, because that sort of information sticks. But it was curtains for Phil. Nick stood by him until he got him absolved, but then he kicked him out. You can't blame him for that, because he wouldn't have been able to put his trust in Phil again.'

'I wouldn't blame him if I thought there was a shred of truth in any of this. I suppose this is a sample of the lies you told Cathy.'

'I didn't have to tell Cathy a thing. She already knew. It couldn't be kept from her. I merely tried to point out to her that until she admitted the facts and found it in her heart to forgive, she was never going to rid herself of her bitterness, and that it would go on eating her up and ruining her life.'

'No, Greg. You're the one who's wrong. Your loyalty to Nick and the admiration you feel for him for what he's made of himself have blinded you to the truth. Phil couldn't have done what you say,' she sobbed, almost beside herself.

'No! It's exactly as I told you. I didn't want to tell you, remember; you made me.'

She turned her head, unmoved by the entreaty in his eyes. He grabbed her by the shoulders, as if he felt the need to shake her to make her see reason. She pulled away, and he dragged her back.

'Let me go!'

'Not in the state you're in. You're distraught, Lindsay. I know it's been a shock to you, but you've got to pull yourself together. Calm down and then I'll let—'

'Take your hands off me,' she screamed.

She heard the click of the door opening before she spoke, but not soon enough for her brain to signal her mouth to close. Her startled eyes saw Nick bearing down on them.

'You heard what she said!' Nick bellowed, eyes blazing as he reached out to hoist Greg to his feet.

Greg didn't have the physique to fight back even if he'd wanted to. He submitted, pleading plaintively, 'You've got it wrong, Nick. I swear it. We were talking, and things got a bit overheated, but it's not what you think. I wasn't making a pass.'

Letting him go with a force that sent Greg reeling across the room, Nick commanded, 'Get out while you can. I want to hear what Lindsay has to say, and if it isn't to my liking it will be in your best interest not to be around for a while. Don't think you're getting away with anything. I intend to deal with you later when I feel more rational.'

'Yes, Nick, just as you say.' Casting a look at Lindsay, the faintest gleam of apology in his eyes for leaving her to deal with Nick's anger, Greg left the room.

Nick moved; two long strides brought him directly in front of her. Even when she was standing he towered over her, and now that she was sitting on the sofa his height seemed especially intimidating. She wanted to cover her eyes and cry. She couldn't take any more; she felt as if she were sinking under the weight of her own tumultuous emotions. Whichever way she went, a man dear to her was going to be discredited. She couldn't believe those dreadful things of Phil. But it was equally inconceivable to imagine that Nick had used her brother as a scapegoat, which was the only alternative. Logic told her that this wasn't possible, yet she wasn't ready to admit to herself that Phil had been disloyal to the man who had elevated him to a position of importance in his organization, paying him a more than generous salary. Furthermore, she couldn't believe that Phil had been unfaithful to the wife he'd professed to love. It was a mire of horror.

To add to her confusion and chilling dismay was the cool violence in Nick's restrained voice as he said, 'I sent Greg packing because I didn't want him to hear what I have to say to you. I saw what was going on between you two before you lured him out. What the devil do you think you're doing?'

As cowardly as it had seemed, Greg's getting out while the going was good was understandable. She couldn't imagine anyone attempting to stand up to this implacable stranger who was a million times removed from the passionate lover who had held her in his arms.

Her teeth almost chattered as she said, 'What are you talking about? I didn't lure him out.'

'You mean it was Greg's idea for you to sneak in here together?'

'No, it wasn't. I asked him to come in here with me. But there was nothing sneaky about it. I had something to ask him.'

'What?'

'Stop trying to browbeat me! Give me one good reason why I should tell you!'

Lindsay wanted to tell him to go to the devil, that she didn't have to explain a thing to him and that she wasn't going to. She wanted to be cool and aloof and sweep out of the room in disdain, but didn't for two reasons. She didn't think her legs would carry her, and if somehow she could manage to conjure up the strength, she didn't think she'd be allowed to get very far.

'I am not trying to beat you down.'

'I should think I'm the best judge of that.'

'Lindsay, I'm a patient man. Where you're concerned I surprise myself at the amount of forbearance I can command, but don't press your luck too far. You can't stall indefinitely. I'll get it out of you no matter what means I have to resort to.'

Would he really resort to physical violence, which was what he was threatening? She decided not to put him to the test.

'I had to ask Greg about Phil. I wanted to know the truth.'

'And he told you?'

Lindsay was quite proud of the way she met

168

that steely gaze. 'He told me quite a lot. I've yet to work it out in my mind whether I think it was the truth or not.'

'I see.' His tone, sounding suddenly brimful of the patience he claimed to have, gave no clue of what he was thinking. 'And if, in your estimation, Greg lied to you, what do you think the truth is?'

He was certainly blunt. She had an answer, but did she dare to tell him? It had taken her forever to figure it out, but now she knew: If Phil hadn't been at fault, then he'd been used to cover up someone else's wild carryings-on.

With that someone staring morosely down at her, a storm warning in his tropical blue eyes, it was difficult for her to speak, but she managed it.

'You were pretty quick to befriend Cathy, or at least your minion was, under your instructions.' She felt cheap referring to Greg as a minion, but it had more impact that way. 'Was it to salve a guilty conscience, Nick? It would have been easy to shift the blame onto Phil for something you did.'

She knew that she had gone too far in saying that. Why she'd said it she didn't know. Something had goaded her into it, despite the fact that she didn't really believe it.

She'd pushed him too far, and she expected some retaliation. She wouldn't have thought much of Nick if he'd let it go. It took a lot of steel for her not to flinch at the anger that flashed across his face. Even worse was the cold contempt that replaced it.

'I'll pretend that you didn't say that,' he gritted. 'You don't need me to tell you how disappointed I am in you.'

No, she didn't. It was no more than she expected. She was disappointed in herself, but no way was she going to hang her head in shame. She was big enough to admit that she was wrong, but she wasn't going to admit it to him, not while he was bullying.

Her eyes were bright and defiant as she said, 'For me the party has just ended. I'll say goodnight.'

'Get your coat. I'll see you home.'

'Thanks, but I won't trouble you. I'd rather someone else took me. Anybody but you. Better still, I'll call a cab.'

She wanted to put some distance between them to think things out, and perhaps even shed the tears lurking behind her eyes, which she couldn't do with Nick Farraday looking on.

His expression was as obdurate as hers; the words that were like bullets shot out of a mouth that barely opened to inform her, 'I don't shelve my responsibilities.'

'You're not responsible for me,' she contested.

He gave her a scathing look. 'There's enough dissent between us without getting into an argument about that. My interest in you has been reported in the press. That makes you

170

extremely vulnerable, and you will remain so until the issue has been decided one way or the other.'

'You mean about the Allure promotion?'

His shrug could have meant anything. He didn't speak for several seconds, as though weighing something in his mind. Then he said, 'We might decide that the few ripples the leak caused are too minor to bother about, in which case the promotion will go ahead. If the alternative decision is reached, the whole thing will be dropped. And I don't give a damn that you have a contract. I'd advise you to read the fine print before considering suing.'

'We really do have a high opinion of each other, don't we, Nick?' she asked with heavy sarcasm. 'Or perhaps you know better, and it's your way of getting back at me by suggesting I'd demand payment for work I hadn't done? Now I'm disappointed in you.'

'So that makes us even,' he mocked. 'And I'm still taking you home.'

She clenched her teeth tightly. 'I still don't know why you feel responsible for me.'

'Someday I might tell you. Now, get your coat.'

She balked at being bossed like that, but nevertheless she did as she was told. It wasn't until she was in his car, his hands on the steering wheel and his concentration on the road, that she muttered rebelliously, 'Someday you're going to meet someone who isn't going to stand for your dictatorial ways, and then you'll get your comeuppance.'

'I'll let you into a secret; I already have.'

'Someone besides Luisa,' she retorted.

He made no answer, but then, she hadn't expected one. Neither of them made any attempt at conversation for the rest of the journey.

'You don't have to see me to my door,' she said in a decisive voice that she hoped he would heed. Wasn't the trick to sound positive?

'I don't have to, but I'm going to. Not only that, I'm going to see you safely inside. And then . . .'

'And then?' she asked in a voice that scraped rawly up from her throat.

'You have no cause for alarm. I'm not going to make violent love to you, no matter how much that would please me. Why are you looking so startled?'

'I've every right to look startled. That's not the sort of thing one says.'

'You mean about it pleasing me to make violent love to you? In other words, the thought is permissible, but the airing of it isn't?'

'One isn't always in control of one's thoughts,' Lindsay admitted rashly, without quite realizing what she was admitting to.

'Do you have those kinds of thoughts?'

'Of course not! And if I do,' she said in

172

contradiction, 'I don't have them where you're concerned.'

She was so disturbed by the turn of the conversation, and by her own confusion, she didn't utter another word until they were outside her door. She didn't like his being there one tiny bit, but the situation seemed to be out of her control. She hurt inside. True or not, Greg Hammond's revelation had shaken her more than she cared to admit. She wanted to be alone, yet she didn't know how to bar Nick from entering her apartment.

She made a feeble attempt to slip in first. 'Good night, Nick.'

The door she was determinedly closing on him was thrust open, and she found herself having to back away from it. In terms of sheer physical strength she was decidedly no match for him, although as their eyes locked, something in his seemed to cringe even as they remained steadily on hers, as if he were regretting being the cause of her fury and defiance.

'I've told you that I'm not going to do anything you wouldn't want me to do,' he spat out in a grim voice.

Was that the crux of the matter? Was it not he at all, but what she wanted him to do, that was frightening her? Everything about him hypnotized her senses. She was held in thrall by his warmth and masculinity, and betrayed by the earthy primitiveness of her own

173

unbidden thoughts. Her tongue was relatively easy to tame, but it was getting increasingly difficult to control her wild imagination. There was a febrile desire in her that was appealing to him to overcome her feeble qualms and her equally feeble excuses and take her even if lust was all he felt for her.

'Greg should be keelhauled for telling you.' Although Nick's eyes were still grim, his tone was noticeably softer. 'After all, Phil was your brother. And any truth that causes suffering should be put under padlock. I feel kind of helpless, Lindsay.'

'You?'

'If you'd fallen and grazed your knees, I could bathe them for you and smear on a dab of soothing antiseptic.' The thought of having her knees bathed and balmed, as if she were a little girl, brought a smile to her lips. 'But I don't know what to do about a bruised heart.'

'I'll be fine, really I will,' Lindsay said, thinking how absurd it was for her to be comforting him.

'Even though I denied having a guilty conscience, that isn't strictly true. I do feel guilty for not showing Phil more tolerance. I didn't understand the forces that could grip a man and make him take something that doesn't rightfully belong to him.'

'Thank you for saying that, Nick. But if Phil did what you say, what Greg told me, then he was wrong.' Why was she saying if? There was no if about it. She knew that if Nick said so, Phil had done these things. 'Something that's been stolen might give fleeting pleasure, but it doesn't bring lasting happiness. Everything worthwhile in this life has got to be earned.'

A troubled look came to Nick's face, but if Lindsay saw it, she wasn't conscious of it; she was too self-involved to bother about any thoughts of his. She knew that she was going to have to earn Nick's forgiveness for thinking what she had about him, and she was going to have to rise above filial devotion to Phil. Why was Nick looking at her in such a strange way? Couldn't he see how desperately she wanted him to put his arms round her and make love to her? But she was forgetting—you didn't get things because you wanted them; you had to earn them. It might take time for him to come to regard her with affection again. But . . . what if it never happened? Having to wait until he came round was bad enough, but to wait in vain forever would be unbearable.

What impulse now drove her she would never know. She took a step forward, stood on tiptoe, and wound her fingers round his neck, bringing herself where she wanted to be, where she felt she belonged—in the circle of his arms.

For a moment his arms formed a protective wing hovering about her; then they closed down, folding her to him. Her soft, desirable lips parted in readiness, delighting his eyes with their moist invitation before he claimed them, taking hungrily of what was so readily given. As the kiss deepened, his tongue intimately foraged the sensuous warmth of her mouth, turning it into a cavern of mutual delight. A wild sweetness exploded between them as her tongue dared to flick briefly against his.

The boldness of her tongue activated her fingers. She tugged at his tie, loosening it and casting it aside so that she could deal with the buttons on his shirt, easing them from their slots. After seeking under his shirt, she slid her hands over his muscled chest, losing her fingertips in the coarse growth of hair.

He in turn assisted her to slide her dress from her shoulders and down over the tautened plane of her stomach and the delicately jutting bones of her hips. As the dress fell his eyes reveled in the lace and satin that covered her creamy breasts. The brilliant-blue density of his eyes glazed over as he unfastened the clasp of her bra and filled his hands with her breasts. His fingers exulted in the silky texture of her skin as they moved over the luxurious curves, enticing them to peak for the brush of his lips. The caress was gentle at first, a tingling, teasing warmth of feeling; then a searing fire inflamed her senses as the pressure increased. She wasn't merely receptive—she craved the touch of his hands and tongue.

As his tongue snaked over and round her excited nipple, she clung to him, her nails digging into his shoulders; she wished in wild abandonment that they were sinking into his flesh, not having to penetrate through the restraining material of his jacket. She didn't want any restraints between them. She wanted to be everything to him.

As one delight ended, another began. The rosy, aureoled points of her breasts were crushed against the hard wall of his chest as his mouth returned to hers. Their breath mingled, and passion took over, inducing him to even greater boldness, sweeping her into a richer lushness of feeling. She was drowning in pure velvet sensuality.

They were hovering on the very borderline of control. Lindsay closed her eyes, weak and dizzy, wondering why he didn't take her.

'What you do to me,' Nick groaned. 'This is . . .'

'. . . ecstasy,' she finished for him.

'No . . . wrong! It's all wrong! God only knows how desperately I need it! But I can't take it. I have to deny myself. I'm not interested in fleeting pleasure. You might hate me for this now, but you'll be glad about it afterward. That's a promise.'

'You're not . . . going, are you?' she asked, dumb-struck.

He seemed to be doing a lot of gulping. His grin was anguished. 'I don't want to, and believe me, this is a first for me, but I've got to do the right thing.' He turned on his heel, stuffing his tie into his pocket and fastening his shirt as he went.

Helplessly she watched him go, berating herself for being such a fool. Her blindness to his needs had ruined everything between them. Once she had begun to think rationally, why hadn't she told Nick that she believed him, that she had been shocked by her brother's deception? She hadn't been thinking coherently. If she'd been in her right senses she would have known that Nick wasn't capable of what she had been accusing him of. He was too honorable to have used her brother, or any man, as a scapegoat to cover his own misdeeds. Nick had been so sickened by her evaluation of him that even though he had responded to her physically, he wasn't able to bring himself to make love to her. He had fought the primitive force of his desire in order to be at peace with his own conscience. She had disgusted him; he would never want to see her again.

Chapter Eight

Lindsay woke to the insistent ringing of the telephone. Could it be Nick calling to give her one more chance? She almost tripped over her own feet in her haste to answer the call.

The keenness of her disappointment upon not hearing Nick's voice was obvious in the flatness of her greeting. 'Oh, hello, Cathy.'

'You don't sound very chirpy,' her sister-in-law informed her.

'I didn't sleep very well,' Lindsay admitted. 'I feel somewhat fragile this morning.'

'You sound it. I thought champagne wasn't supposed to give you a hangover, or were you mixing your drinks?' A sharper note entered Cathy's voice. 'Or couldn't you sleep because of a guilty conscience over the way you set me up?'

'What do you mean?' Lindsay asked cautiously.

'You didn't tell me that Greg Hammond would be at the party. That was sneaky. You know he's not one of my favorite people.'

'I'm not the only one who's been secretive. There are things you haven't told me about Phil.'

'Whom have you been talking to?'

'I got it out of Greg Hammond. I was tired of being in the dark about Phil. You could have warned me, Cathy. I walked straight into it; it was like hitting a brick wall.'

'Perhaps I didn't tell you because I knew you'd believe their version.'

'Is there another version, Cathy?' Lindsay asked wearily. 'The thing that puzzles me is why Phil acted the way they say he did. I don't know, but I'm getting a strong feeling that more than envy and avarice pushed him to pass himself off as Nick Farraday.' She waited hopefully, but the pause lengthened until it became apparent that Cathy wasn't going to enlighten her. On this subject Cathy was no help to her, sticking resolutely to firmly-held convictions. Sighing, Lindsay said, 'Honestly, I didn't see it as a set-up last night. And I had the wrong impression about you and Greg Hammond. But from what I saw, you didn't have much difficulty in avoiding him, not with Jim Bourne monopolizing you.'

'All right, so I'm not as angry with you as I could have been.'

'So you didn't phone to blast my eardrums?'

'I couldn't let it pass without saying something; but no, not really. I'm going shopping this morning for clothes. That old complaint, I've nothing to wear, is the absolute truth. I've neglected myself terribly. I was wondering if you'd like to come with me, perhaps offer some frank opinions.'

Lindsay wondered if Cathy's revived interest in appearance had anything to do with the attention Jim Bourne had paid her. She herself could use the company; a shopping spree was infinitely better than a day spent moping by herself.

And so, cheered by Cathy's brightness, she said, 'I'd love to come.'

*   *   *

Cathy's newfound energy left Lindsay gasping all day. When they had finished, Lindsay felt as though she didn't want to look at another dress or blouse or skirt or pair of shoes ever again. Hours later, exhausted, they put down their parcels and rested their weary bodies in their favourite seafood restaurant. Lindsay hadn't been totally successful in unburdening herself of her thoughts; her mind had kept returning to Nick Farraday and the revelations about Phil, and she only toyed with the mouthwatering platter set before her.

'Poor old you,' Cathy sympathized. 'You really are out of sorts. It was cruel of me to drag you out today.'

'It wasn't,' Lindsay said, making a valiant effort to eat a prawn. 'And it's a joy to see you taking an interest in yourself again and looking so much better. Yesterday's party did you good.'

'I agree. I'm glad you invited me, and thanks for persevering with me all this time. I'd forgotten what it was like to have fun.'

'It was good to see you enjoying yourself. You and Jim Bourne seemed to get on well.'

'Yes, we did. But don't go making too much of it.'

'Oh? I thought that was the reason for your resumed interest in life.'

'In a way it is. I felt comfortable with him,

181

and that in itself seemed like a miracle.'

'I don't know what's so miraculous about it. Jim Bourne is one of the easiest people I know to get along with.'

'He might be, but he's a man. And I haven't been easy with men since . . . since Stephanie's birth.' A debate seemed to be going on behind Cathy's eyes; then her chin tilted at an angle of defiance. 'I went off that side of marriage. You might not take kindly to hearing this, but here goes. Your brother was a fine man in many ways, but patience wasn't his strong point.'

Lindsay didn't know how to answer that. Cathy hadn't had an easy time giving birth to Stephanie, and naturally she would have wanted time before resuming a sexual relationship again. Was Cathy saying that Phil had tried to rush her, and in doing so had put her off of sex? That, of course, would explain why Phil had gone astray: When he couldn't get affection from his wife, he had started seeing other women.

Lindsay shook her head in a gesture of perplexity and said in genuine surprise, 'I never suspected there was anything wrong between you.'

'Wrong?' Cathy contested. 'There's more to marriage than sex. A man can arrange that. And we had so much going for us. Shared pastimes and interests, and a deep caring for each other that never wavered.' A return of the old bitterness sparked in the melting sadness of her eyes. 'If Phil had been given more time, I know that things would have sorted themselves out.'

'Oh, Cathy,' Lindsay despaired. Cathy was still vindictive toward Nick Farraday for what she considered to be his part in Phil's death. How misguided she was! Couldn't she see that the tragedy that had occurred had been the result of their own shortcomings, hers and Phil's? Perhaps she didn't want to see . . . Perhaps she dared not see the truth because it might weigh too heavily on her conscience.

The final piece of the puzzle had clicked into place for Lindsay—the reason why Phil had sought the company of other women. There was no guarantee that her weak and fun-loving brother wouldn't have succumbed anyway, but the odds had gone heavily against him once Cathy had barred him from her bed following Stephanie's birth. Why hadn't Cathy been more reasonable and understood that a man couldn't wait indefinitely? Why hadn't Phil been more patient and understanding with Cathy and earned his way back into her bed with tender caring?

'I'm glad things are better for you,' Lindsay said generously.

'Yes, so am I. I don't know if anything will develop between me and Jim, but that's not the important point. What *is* important is the way I felt last night. We talked and danced, and I didn't freeze up on him. Not only that, I found myself responding to a man. It's been such a long time, I'd forgotten what it was like to have those kinds of feelings.'

'As I said, I'm glad for you, Cathy. I truly am. We should have talked sooner.'

Soon enough for Lindsay to have salvaged some happiness for herself.

The following day she thought about going round to see Nick and try to put things right. She spent almost the entire morning rehearsing things to say, but nothing sounded appropriate.

When the phone rang and, on lifting the receiver, she heard his voice, she said hurriedly, 'I was going to ring you, only I couldn't think of anything to say.'

'That does sound like a logical reason for not ringing. If you didn't have anything to say, there wouldn't have been much point in calling, would there?'

'No, I suppose not.' Why hadn't she let him say why he was phoning her?

'I tried to phone you yesterday, during the day. I was tied up last night. A business dinner that went on and on.'

She wondered if his secretary, the cool and luscious Barbara Bates, had accompanied him. 'I was out . . . with Cathy. We went on a shopping spree—for her, not for me, although I did see one dress I couldn't resist. And then Cathy treated me to lunch.'

'And no doubt injected you with another

dose of her poison about me.'

'No, Nick, although we did talk. I admit that in the past I've swallowed too much of her poison, but not anymore. And yesterday I got a clearer picture of things, a better understanding of what motivated Phil. Even though I don't condone what he did, at least I can understand why he did it. I can even see the reasoning behind Cathy's misguided attitude.'

'That's progress, to admit that you consider her attitude misguided.'

'Did you want something special, Nick?' Lindsay asked, a great sadness engulfing her at Nick's polite, clipped tone. He was too formal, too far away.

'I wanted to tell you that I know you weren't responsible for the leak in the Hot Sauce column.'

'You know I wasn't!' Lindsay's breath rushed out of her. 'That implies that you know who *was*!'

'Yes. The culprit owned up. It was Luisa.'

'Why would she do such a thing? Of course! She didn't want me in the first place, so she thought that if she let something get out, you would have to drop me.' She frowned. It was obvious that Luisa was the kind of woman who liked to get her own way, but it was unthinkable that she would resort to such tactics. Furthermore, wasn't Luisa her friend? 'Luisa didn't know we'd been dancing together,' Lindsay pointed out.

'No. But Maisie Pellman's spies are everywhere. Everything I do is considered an interesting tidbit. She would have known that I'd been seen dancing somewhat intimately with a blonde—and made the natural connection. Luisa had another reason for doing what she did besides wanting you off the promotion.'

'Oh?'

'I think we should talk about it, but not over the phone.'

'About whether I'm on or off the promotion? Do you want me to come round to your office?'

'No, my office isn't the place, either. In any case, I've got a fairly heavy schedule. What color is it?'

'What color is what?'

'The dress you bought.'

'Oh . . . multicolored. Yellow and pink and blue.'

'Would you like to give it an airing this evening? I'd like to take you out for a meal. We could talk things over then.'

'Yes, all right.'

'I'll call for you around seven-thirty.'

'Fine.'

She put down the receiver, wondering how it was possible to be both jubilant and sad at the same time. She was happy at the thought of seeing Nick again, but her heart was

186

breaking at the gulf his politeness had put between them. She knew what he was leading up to. He was going to tell her that she was off the promotion, she was certain of that. After tonight she might never see him again.

How often she'd gibed at his pompous, overbearing manner; how ironic that it was *that* Nick whom she wanted back! She didn't know this polite stranger at all, this Nick who was intent on pushing her out of his life.

For the rest of the day she couldn't concentrate on anything; she longed for the moment when she could start getting ready. Driven by her own impatience, and remembering that the last time he'd come early, she began her preparations much too soon and was ready by six-thirty. Silly of her, because she didn't know how well her new dress would stand up to wrinkles, and she didn't want to sit for long and spoil its crisp freshness.

She prowled around, her living room seeming more cramped than ever. But it wasn't as crowded as the thoughts rushing round in her brain. She kept thinking how wonderful she had felt in Nick's arms, and she wondered at the control he'd exercised to draw back from the brink of love-making. It was all her fault. She'd held back too long, and she'd lost him.

A knock sounded on the door and her eyes went to the clock. It was still a quarter short of seven, and Nick had said seven-thirty. She was right in thinking that he'd be early, but he was even earlier than she'd expected.

She raced to open the door, her smile of welcome freezing into politeness when she saw not Nick, but two men she'd never set eyes on before. One was tall and dark haired. The other man, though shorter, was the more thick-set of the two, and he had sandy-colored hair.

She couldn't explain why, but a feeling of deep unease ran through her. She cast a hasty glance down the stairs and along the passageway to the next apartment, her heart dropping when she saw no one about.

'I'm sorry, but whatever it is you're selling, I'm not interested in buying,' she said in firm dismissal.

'Selling? We're not selling anything, lady,' the dark-haired man said, the smile on his lips chilling her.

'What do you want?' she asked in as cool and collected a voice as she could muster.

'Just for you to come for a ride with us.'

'No way!'

She attempted to slam the door in their smirking faces, but the sandy-haired man moved forward to impose his bulk in the doorway.

His friend, who seemed to have taken on the job of spokesman, said, 'You don't understand. I'm not asking you, I'm telling you.'

'And I'm telling the pair of you to get lost. What in heaven's name is this all about?'

'I'll explain everything as we go, lady, if I decide explanation is necessary.'

Things came flooding back to her. At the very beginning, when Nick's interest in her had been purely business, he'd said something about moving her into an apartment where she'd be protected. 'You'll be a hot property. As such you'll require some form of protection,' he'd said. And more recently he had murmured about the piece in the Hot Sauce column making her vulnerable. Was this what he had meant?

Was this an attempted kidnapping? She couldn't see how these men had figured out that she was of any value, but yes, this was a kidnap bid!

'No!' Lindsay gasped in stunned disbelief. It was too ludicrous. She'd been watching too much television. It couldn't be.

'Oh, yes, lady,' the dark-haired man said. 'I figured you for an intelligent chick. I knew you'd get there eventually.'

'But why?'

'Money. What else?'

'I know that. But there won't be any money in this.'

'No? That's just your opinion. It's our belief that Nick Farraday will pay handsomely.'

'No, he won't. His interest in me was leaked to the press. I'm off the promotion now. But

189

even if that weren't so, you wouldn't get any ransom for me. I'm not that valuable. Another girl would be assigned in my place.'

'Sorry, lady. Good try. But we have it on the best authority that Nick Farraday's interest in you is the kind of business done between the sheets. Apparently you're special enough to him that he'll pay whatever we ask. No accounting for taste, though; I go for a well-stacked chick every time, myself.'

The sandy-haired man spoke for the first time. 'Cut the talk. We're wasting time.'

Wasting time was just what Lindsay wanted. Every moment they delayed brought Nick nearer. She just prayed that he would be early, that he'd get there soon enough to save her. She didn't know what price they'd put on her, or whether Nick would pay up before calling the police in. She thought the latter possibility more likely. Nick wasn't the type to be intimidated by thugs. But where would that leave her? Even when a ransom was paid, kidnap victims didn't always escape with their lives. She was suddenly very, very frightened.

'Please go away. I won't report this, and I promise not to remember your faces, if you'll just leave.'

Oh, God, why hadn't they covered their faces? And why had she just said such a dumb thing? She knew that they weren't going to depart quietly, and that she'd just signed her death warrant by drawing attention to the fact that she could identify them.

Squaring her jaw at them, Lindsay said, 'You won't get away with it. You can't believe you'll be able to walk out of this building without fuss. Someone's bound to be about, and I'm not going to go quietly. Use your common sense, *please.*'

'Use yours, lady. If you love thy neighbor, as the good book tells you to, you'll be as quiet as the grave. Otherwise you'll assist anyone who tries to stop us into their own grave. You see, I've got a little friend in my pocket who'll help. I'm not a man of violence, and I'll only use my gun if provoked, so don't provoke me,' he advised menacingly.

Not a man of violence indeed! He was enjoying this; they both were!

She refused to let them know how scared she was. 'Don't quote the Bible to me, you heathen.'

She felt sick, and her nausea increased tenfold as they each grabbed an arm and began to hustle her out.

'At least let me get my coat.'

But was she wise in stalling? She wanted Nick to get there in time to know what was happening to her, but she didn't want him to get hurt. Her abductor might have been bluffing when he said he was armed, but then again, he might not have been. This was rather an audacious scheme, and they must have had some reason to think they could pull it off.

191

The sinking feeling in her stomach increased as she realized the probability that they were both carrying weapons of some sort. Nick wouldn't stand a chance against two armed and desperate men.

'You don't need a coat. We'll put the heater on in the car. You can have it just as hot as you want, lady.' She read in his eyes exactly what he meant, even before he put it into words. 'If you don't make a murmur, you won't get hurt. You'll have a nice comfortable hideout until your boyfriend pays up.'

I'll bet, Lindsay gritted silently. She was suddenly more furious than she was frightened. She certainly wasn't going to let them take her without putting up a fight. She kicked all the way down the stairs and tried to bite the hand that was clamped over her mouth to prevent her from screaming. Most of her kicks missed, but at least two landed on target and brought grunts of pain. It was a miracle, or a misfortune, that they managed to keep their balance and that she didn't bring all three of them crashing down the stairs.

'I told you it was lunacy. We should have bided our time,' the taller man said.

'And let this fish slip through the net? Remember, we were told to act fast. Just leave it to me,' his sandy-haired friend replied.

Lindsay wasn't left long to ponder about what he meant. Something crashed against the back of her head, leaving her just short of unconscious. As she slumped, her stomach froze at the cruelty and ruthless determination of her captors.

The rest of the nightmare flight down the stairs and into the street passed in a painful haze. She was aware of people passing them, but no one stopped to help her. Instead, they just walked on, minding their own business. Wasn't anyone curious to know why two men were propping up one worse-for-wear female? She tried to call out, to make someone pay attention. She felt as if she were shouting, but only a trace of sound came from her mouth.

'You all right, miss?' someone finally asked.

'No . . . call . . .'

'Thanks, buddy, but she's okay,' one of the thugs, the dark-haired one, cut in. 'Bit of a celebration. A drop too much to drink. You know how it is.'

'Don't I just!'

'She'll be as right as rain once we get her home.'

The man was taken in. In a second he was gone.

They had now stopped by a car apparently belonging to the thugs.

'You'll be fine now, honey. We'll soon have you home, and then you'll be able to sleep it off,' the dark-haired one said, keeping up the charade.

Someone chuckled and called out jovially, 'Rather her than me. Wouldn't want her hangover when she wakes up.'

And then a noise, a commotion, alerted her to glance farther along the pavement. Miraculously, she saw Nick running toward them, knocking people out of the way in his haste. They wouldn't shoot him down and add murder to their crime, she speculated, not with so many people there to witness the offense. Her heart hammering, she made one last attempt to free herself, feeling that her prayers had been answered. But she was worn out. Her strength lagged sadly behind her will, and her madly struggling body was thrown into the back of the car. The dark-haired man came in beside her, and his partner in crime took the wheel.

He wouldn't be able to move until a gap appeared to let him into the moving stream of cars. She prayed that the traffic would stay bumper-to-bumper. The sandy-haired man pulled on the steering wheel, intent on forcing his way out. He wasn't waiting for his chance; he was creating it. A slamming on of brakes from the car behind and he was in. The noisy revving of the car engine filled her ears. Nick was so close now, but not close enough. She gulped down her dismay and anguish. He couldn't possibly save her now.

Surely, though, he would be alert enough to take the car's license plate number and notify the police. But somehow she felt that the thugs had guarded against that happening. She wouldn't be at all surprised to find that there was another car waiting for them before they'd travelled very far. The sandy-haired man had said, 'Remember, we were told to act fast'—indicating that someone else was involved. Her mind spun at the hopelessness of her predicament.

What happened then was even more incredible than the events so far. She saw Nick cut through the moving traffic and take a flying leap into the air. Then his face appeared at the windshield. He had actually jumped onto the hood of the car, and was blocking the driver's visibility while hanging on for grim death. It could very well *be* grim death—his own!

There was a jangled squeal of brakes and a grinding of mangled metal, punctuated by obscenities shouted out by her two captors. Then everything faded as she fell into a black pit of unconsciousness.

She edged back into awareness with the realization that her face and body were throbbing painfully, and that she was still in the back of the car. Now, however, the arm round her shoulders wasn't restraining her, but comforting her. She looked up, in her muzziness expecting to see Nick's dear and familiar features. Her heart all but stopped at the sight of a stranger's face.

'Who are you?'

'The name's Cliff. I was passing by and

volunteered to stay with you.'

Tears streamed down her cheeks. She was sure Nick was dead. He couldn't possibly have done what he had and still be alive. The crazy, heroic fool! Why hadn't he let her take her chances? What good was life if he wouldn't be there to share it with her?

'Where do you hurt?' Cliff asked in deep concern.

'Inside.'

'A doctor will be here soon.'

She shook her head. 'No, not that kind of hurt. Nick . . . He's . . .?' She couldn't bring herself to go on.

'Oh, I understand. If Nick's your man, he's doing fine, and could do better if they'd let him. You don't have to worry about him—or yourself while he's around. It took six guys to hold him back and stop him from beating the hell out of those two hoodlums. But not before he'd managed to drop a couple of nice shots on both of them. I don't think either of those ruffians will ever tangle with him or his ever again.'

Instead of stopping, her tears came faster. The stranger seemed to understand.

'A natural reaction. Let it come. Get it all out of your system. There, there.'

She liked the things the stranger said, the assumption that she belonged to Nick and was under his protection.

Nick suddenly poked his head through the

window and ground out bitingly, 'Lindsay Cooper, you're a menace to my peace of mind.' To Lindsay this playful aggression was like being doused with a bucket of cold water.

The doctor who arrived on the scene took a look at her and agreed with Nick that she should be taken to a hospital. She insisted that she was all right, that she didn't want to go to a hospital, but Nick refused to listen to her protests. He was back to the bullying Nick. And yet, in a strange kind of way, even though the restrained violence about him frightened her, it was better than the formal politeness of the stranger.

At the hospital there were more arguments. She didn't want to stay overnight for observation, but Nick was insistent that she should. 'I'm not going to have more on my conscience than I already do.'

She wanted to ask him if that was all she was to him, a burden on his conscience, but she didn't have the nerve. She didn't feel strong enough to cope with an unfavorable answer.

Nick was shooed out—at least *someone* could boss him, she exclaimed to herself—while she was cleaned up and antiseptic dabbed on the various cuts and scratches she had acquired. Then she was put into a regulation hospital nightgown and popped into bed—in a private room no doubt arranged for by Nick.

Then Nick was allowed back in. 'There's a policeman waiting outside. Do you feel up to talking to him? Let's put it another way. I promise not to let him tire you too much, but I think you should make the effort.'

She nodded. 'All right, I'll go along with that. Nick?'

'Yes?'

'Those two men . . . they didn't get away, did they?' She didn't see how they could have, but after the events of that day nothing would have surprised her.

'No. They're in custody. You'll be called upon to identify them later. For now, tell the policeman all you know. It's possible that they're hired thugs, and that someone else is behind the kidnap plot.'

'I know from what they said that someone else *is* involved.'

'I'd better get the policeman in; otherwise you'll have to go through the ordeal of repeating everything, and I've an idea that once will take enough out of you.'

'You could be right.'

Nick went to tell the policeman that Lindsay would see him, returning with him a short time later. During the session that followed, Nick sat back, arms folded, his face grave as she told everything she knew.

Nick's presence was oddly comforting. But the details of the conversation she'd had with the two men were difficult to repeat in front of

198

him. When the policeman read her statement back to her, she wished her memory hadn't been quite so accurate, especially regarding the bit about Nick's interest in her being the kind between the sheets. When Nick heard this, his lips twitched in a slight smile, though the policeman's expression remained commendably impassive. She did notice that both men seemed to pay more attention to the part about the thug going for the well-stacked chick every time.

'Have you any idea who he was referring to?' the policeman asked.

'I haven't a clue,' Lindsay said truthfully.

'I think I may have,' Nick announced somberly.

'Oh?' said the other man.

'Later. Miss Cooper looks tired.'

That was an understatement.

'I've almost finished, sir. Just a couple more things. Miss Cooper, can you—'

Again Nick intervened. 'She's exhausted. Put your notebook away. If you'll wait outside, I'll be with you shortly.'

The policeman accepted his dismissal. It occurred to Lindsay that he didn't have much choice in the matter. If he hadn't gone of his own choice, she wouldn't have been surprised to see Nick take him by the collar and throw him out.

The moment the door clicked shut, Lindsay's eyes lifted to Nick in gratitude.

'Thanks for cutting it short. I don't think I could have taken much more. What's it all about? Who do you think hired those men to kidnap me?'

'Someone who knew you were special to me and was angry about it. Two people who are close to me were in the know. One is Luisa.'

'But Luisa wouldn't have—'

'Of course not! I'm not suggesting any such thing. Luisa fed Maisie Pellman the tidbit in that column for a reason other than her desire to see you off the Allure promotion. She's fond of you, and I wouldn't like you to get the wrong impression of what motivated her. To get her own way, she doesn't always fight fair.' A crooked smile lifted his mouth. 'After all, she's a woman. But this time she had a magnanimous reason for what she did. She thought it wasn't going to occur to me in time that I was launching you on a career which would put you beyond my reach. The other person who is aware of my feelings for you is also a woman . . .'

The well-stacked female who was more to the kidnapper's taste? Lindsay wondered.

'One I may have underestimated. Time will tell. Don't puzzle your head about it,' Nick instructed. 'I promise you that this will all be sorted out. For now, I've asked the nurse to give you something to make you sleep.'

'I don't want anything. I never take pills.'

'Will you ever stop arguing with me? Do as

200

you're told. I'll come back tomorrow to take you home.'

In spite of his bossiness, his words had a nice ring to them.

Nick kissed her goodnight, his lips lightly brushing her bruised mouth. Seconds after he'd left the nurse came in with a tiny pill and a glass of water. She too looked to be the sort who wouldn't take no for an answer. Just wait, just wait until I feel better, Lindsay thought mutinously. She put the pill in her mouth, but was careful not to swallow it, and removed it the moment the nurse's back was turned. She didn't want to sleep, not yet. Nick had said she was special to him, and she wanted to gloat about that for a while. Their relationship wasn't over . . . he'd said he was coming to take her home . . . she was special to him.

The nurse slipped back into the room to have a look at Lindsay.

'You're not asleep yet, Miss Cooper,' she chided. 'Perhaps I should give you another sleeping pill to knock you out. Your fiancé isn't going to be pleased with me if I don't see that you get a good night's rest.'

'Nick Farraday isn't my fiancé.'

'He told me he was.'

'You must have been mistaken.'

'No mistake. Your face took quite a beating. You're going to have a real shiner in the morning. Mr. Farraday said it isn't going to look too well in your wedding photographs.'

Chapter Nine

Lindsay opened her eyes to bright sunlight and the realization that not only her face ached, but her entire body. She was hazy about a lot that had happened the previous day, but the bruises she'd sustained on her face and body were vivid reminders that the violence had been very real.

She knew that she was trying to protect herself by wondering if she'd only dreamed the special moments of the previous night. Nick *had* said she was special. Yet surely the nurse had mistaken Nick's statements about marriage and wedding photographs. Or maybe she herself had just mistaken what the nurse said.

Nick was anti-marriage. He hadn't been able to leave fast enough the night she'd assumed wedding bells were inevitably in the offing. And if that weren't enough, her beliefs concerning his blame in Phil's downfall had so sickened him that he hadn't been able to make love to her.

Lindsay wanted to leave the hospital straight after breakfast, but the nurses wouldn't allow her, insisting that she didn't realize the ordeal she'd been through, that she had to rest quietly now. She didn't ask whose orders these were, fearing that she was a prisoner of Nick's whim.

It was late afternoon before Nick came for her. His clothes matched his eyes—blue slacks and a deeper blue shirt. The shirt's open neck showed off the strong column of his throat. The designer slacks hugged his lean hips and long legs, emphasizing their muscled strength. The nurses couldn't keep their eyes off him, and neither could she. He looked gorgeous.

They'd allowed her to wash her hair. She'd arranged it so that its pale gold silkiness floated against her cheeks, not to achieve the wild and wanton look, but as a partial covering for the worst of her bruises. The nurse who'd been looking after her had had her dress laundered, but it hadn't ironed very well. All in all, she felt a mess.

Yet as Nick's eyes swept over her, even taking note of the heavy bruising, that wasn't the aspect they were registering. She knew that even now she still attracted him physically, and that if they'd been in a love-making situation, he wouldn't have held back this time.

'Ready?' he inquired.

She said sedately, 'I've been ready to go home since first thing this morning. What kept you?'

'Sorry about that. I seem to have been tied up with officialdom for most of the day.'

'You're here now, so I'll let you off. Any developments?'

'A few. Let's get you home first; then we

can talk.'

'If I've got a home to go to. Those two thugs didn't allow me time for anything, so the apartment's been unlocked all night.'

'No, it hasn't. I realized as much, and went straight to your place after leaving you to make certain that everything was secure.'

'Thanks. You think of everything.'

'Not always. Sometimes I slip up quite badly. There was something else I thought of, though. I didn't imagine you'd want to go out for a meal, and I didn't particularly relish the idea either. I don't fancy having it reported in the Hot Sauce column that I beat my woman up, and that really is some shiner you've got. So I brought all the necessary ingredients for a meal. I trust you approve?'

He had said 'my woman.' She hadn't dreamed *that*.

She nodded. 'Yes, I approve.'

'Good,' he said simply, taking her arm.

As he put her into his car she felt cherished. She supposed that that wasn't the place for a serious talk, so she repressed her natural curiosity about recent events until they got home. They didn't talk much at all until they entered her apartment building.

'Were you scared?' he asked as they walked up the stairs, the same ones she'd been cruelly hustled down the day before.

'You want the truth? I was petrified!'

After locking up the previous night, he'd

pocketed her key. He shifted the bag that contained their meal to his left hand so he could take the key from his pocket and open the door. She walked in, thinking how strange it was that everything looked so normal. It seemed cruelly impersonal that the apartment bore no imprint of the previous day's violence.

Nick went through to the kitchen to dump the bag on the counter. She sank into a chair, leaving 'his' chair for him.

On coming back, he didn't immediately sit down; instead, he simply stood and looked solemnly at her.

'Oh . . . Lindsay.'

Cringing uncomfortably under his solicitous concentration, she said, 'I'll remember yesterday fifty years after I'm dead. It couldn't have happened in Haworth. People there have a healthy regard for what's happening around them. Was anyone hurt?'

Apparently she hadn't deflected him, because he said, 'You mean, apart from you? When I saw what those monsters were doing to you, I wanted to tear them apart with my bare hands. Perhaps it was lucky I was pulled off or I'd have murdered them.'

'Cliff, the passerby who was in the car with me when I came round, said that you were having a good try.'

He nodded in grim satisfaction. 'You're not the only one who'll be nursing a sore jaw for a day or two. I just wish that I'd been given

205

longer with them.'

'I asked for a lot of what I got. I lashed out instead of going quietly as they advised me to.'

'You didn't lash out hard enough.'

She grinned. 'You weren't in my shoes.'

Either he didn't hear her, or didn't believe her, because he said, 'I see I'll have to teach you the art of self-defense.' He paused. 'Although I'm about to contradict myself, it might have been better for you if you hadn't resisted. You wouldn't have had to take the beating you did.'

'But if I hadn't stalled them, you wouldn't have reached me in time.'

'True enough.' His mouth was grim and bitter again. 'It took guts to do what you did.'

With a deep sigh, Lindsay said, 'I couldn't make up my mind whether I was being foolhardy or brave. One of them said he had a little friend in his pocket who'd help. Please tell me he was bluffing.'

'I'd love to oblige, but it would be a lie.'

'Did he . . . use it? I didn't hear any shots, but I suppose it could have been fitted with a silencer.'

'By the time either of them could have pulled a gun, it was all up with them. They've already got criminal records, so they had no wish to add murder to their crimes. Thank God they realized that, because quite a crowd had gathered. It could have ended in tragedy.'

'Yes.' Lindsay swallowed, and it was some

seconds before she could ask, 'What was the extent of the damage?'

'I was blocking the driver's view. He stewed into a couple of cars and they in turn hit others. But no one was injured—not seriously anyway, just minor scratches and one sprained wrist. Nothing happened that the signing of a check won't fix.'

'Did you find out what it was all about? Why they picked me?'

Only then did Nick slump down in the chair, sinking his face in his hands. 'Barbara Bates wasn't at her desk this morning, and she's cleared out of her apartment. That's no coincidence. Her accomplices have sung their heads off and confirmed that she was behind it. A full alert's out for her. She'll be picked up.'

'I knew your secretary didn't like me, but surely trying to have me kidnapped was a bit extreme,' Lindsay said, deciding to be flip again.

'It's no joke, Lindsay.'

'I know, Nick. I'm sorry.'

'You don't have a thing to be sorry about.'

'And neither have you, Nick Farraday.'

'That's a matter of opinion. I've already told you about the showdown we had when it dawned on me that Barbara had the wrong idea about my feelings for her, and I honestly thought that I'd straightened her out. I swear that what I told you was the truth. She was

207

useful when it came to dining and entertaining clients and business associates. Luisa wasn't up to mixing with a lot of people, and there have been occasions when I've asked Barbara into my home to act as my hostess. But I never, ever, considered her as a permanent candidate for the job. By having you kidnapped, she was killing two birds with one stone. She wanted to make me suffer and at the same time get her hands on a sizeable amount of money. She was there when I phoned to arrange to pick you up at seven-thirty. I'd already told her to check with me before making any new appointments, and I'd warned her that I might be cancelling the existing ones. She was astute enough to know why—it was something unprecedented—and she knew she hadn't a moment to lose.'

'Barbara was another Phil,' Lindsay put in sadly. 'Someone else who coveted what wasn't theirs.'

'Poor Phil. I seem to be bad news for you and yours.'

'Phil was wrong, even though it must have seemed to him that circumstances drove him to do what he did. Those other women . . . I know why he turned to them. It seems that Cathy . . . well, after Stephanie was born, things weren't right between her and Phil.'

'I'd no idea at the time, but I've wondered since if he had domestic problems.'

'I'm not blaming Cathy. It's not something a woman wants to happen. But perhaps if they'd sat down and talked things out . . .' She sighed. 'Anyway, you can't blame yourself for anything. Nothing's been your fault.' Her voice didn't sound right, due partly to her hurt mouth, but also to the emotion overcoming her.

'Thanks,' Nick said in a tone that was the twin of hers.

Meeting his eyes, Lindsay said, 'The biggest shock of all was seeing you do that fool leap onto the car. You might have been killed, or maimed for life.'

'Not a chance,' he said lightly. 'It wasn't even a calculated risk. I knew what I was doing.'

'Did you?' Even though a note of admiration had crept into her voice, there was still a hint of something challenging as she went on to say, 'Luisa told me that among other mad things in your daredevil past, you'd been a professional stunt man.'

'So what are you going on about? Jumping onto a moving car is as easy as falling off a house top. It's all a question of knowing how.'

The careless way he tried to shrug off his heroics intensified the feeling of admiration building up inside her. 'No, it isn't. It's a lot more than that. It's precision and timing and practice. You're not going to tell me that you're in practice at jumping on cars. And you had no tricks of the trade to fall back on, like a cozy mattress to break your fall and stop you from breaking your neck if you fell off. You could have been reduced to pulp in that traffic.'

'Have you finished?'

'Not by a long chalk. How old were you when you were a stunt man?'

'Nineteen, twenty. I don't remember exactly,' he replied evasively.

'And how old are you now?'

'What's that got to do with it?'

'How old?' she persisted, then added teasingly, 'What's the matter? Coy about your age?'

He scowled. 'Of course not. I'm thirty-five. That is, I was when I got up yesterday morning. I feel as if I've aged twenty years since then. I don't see what that's got to do with it.'

She held her breath in exasperation. 'Then you're even dumber than I thought. It's got everything to do with it. It's time you slowed down and only tackled things within your capabilities.'

A definite twinkle entered his eyes. 'You wouldn't care to draw a list up of what you consider those capabilities to be?'

Despite herself, her mouth twitched up at the corners. 'No!'

'Then shut up,' he commanded sharply. Then, in a softer tone, he said, 'Were you really concerned about me?'

'Of course I was. I nearly died when I saw what you were doing.'

'I'm sorry if I gave you a fright, but I didn't seem to have much alternative. I didn't have a lot of time to think, either. I was approaching on the other side of the road, in my car, and I was stuck in traffic. I saw those two guys bundling you out of the building as if you were a sack of flour. It was like waving a red rag at a bull. I stopped my car where it was and got out. If you want to know the really tricky part, it was crossing between the moving cars. I almost *did* get myself killed then.'

'Oh, Nick.' She gulped. She wanted to tell him that if he had been killed, she would have wanted to die, too. But she couldn't burden him with that thought.

His eyes had gone tender, and she knew that he still fancied her. He wouldn't fancy every woman he came in contact with, and that made her at least somewhat special. As for his behavior at the hospital, in thinking it over in her mind she'd decided that he'd told the hospital staff that he was her fiancé to cut through red tape.

'We never did get round to having that talk, did we? The reason you wanted to see me yesterday,' she said.

'Don't you know why?'

'Yes. You were all set to tell me that I was off the Allure promotion.'

'Among other things, yes. Yesterday's rumpus has saved me from having to tell you that you're free of all duties concerning the

211

promotion. We've decided to bring the launch date forward, which would have put you out of it in any case. You're not going to 'allure' the public with that bruised face, so you can't possibly put up any objection to someone else being brought in.'

She didn't want to allure the public. She only wanted to allure him. He was getting his own way, so did he have to sound so cheerful about her being ditched? 'No, I can't. What else?'

'What else what?'

'You said among other things,' Lindsay explained.

'Oh, that.' The look Nick sent her shot a red-hot quiver through her system. 'I want you. I can't live without you. There's no fun in anything, no meaning. I'm miserable away from you. I got to doing some serious thinking, and so . . . I have a little something to put to you.' His anxious eyes searched Lindsay's face.

'A proposition?' It came out as a tiny croak.

'Nearly,' he acknowledged. 'You've got the beginning right.'

'The beginning?' Lindsay puzzled. 'Propo— *oh*!'

He nodded.

Her heartbeat took on a most peculiar rhythm. Without saying a word, but doing a lot of swallowing to dissolve the tightness in her throat, she got up and crossed to where he was. She knelt on the floor and slid between

212

his legs, resting her arms on his sturdy thighs.

His hand came out to tangle her hair, welcoming her. 'The wrong one's kneeling,' he said gruffly.

'A proposal? You were going to propose to me?' she said, getting her voice back.

'Mmmm. I don't know why you sound so surprised.'

'You don't? After the way you went off me like you did?'

'Went off you? And just when was that supposed to be?'

'The moment I blurted something out about marriage the other night, I knew I'd written my own exit lines, or I thought I had,' she said, a note of wonder entering her voice.

'You jumped the gun,' Nick said firmly, if not very convincingly.

'Come off it,' she scoffed gently. 'Marriage was the last thing you had in mind. I was, or thought I was, just another conquest to you.'

'I'm sure I would have come round to thinking about marriage,' Nick insisted in a low growl.

'Okay,' she laughed. 'I'll believe you.'

'Will you also believe that I haven't had as many conquests as I've been credited with?'

Somberly she said, 'I imagine that my brother accounted for a few of them.'

'I'm sorrier than I can ever say that you had to know what Phil was up to.'

'Me too. I sickened you when I took Phil's

side. You thought I should have believed you.'

'Yes, for a moment. That was very self-righteous of me. But . . . sickened me, you said? Do you mind telling me how you arrived at that conclusion?'

'I do mind. It's painful. Do I have to?'

'Yes, you do.'

She dropped her chin onto his knee. 'I disappointed you. You said so. You thought I should have taken your word as the truth. I let you down by not having faith in you. I shouldn't have had to think about it; I should have *known*! You were so disgusted with me that you couldn't bring yourself to make love to me. And I couldn't blame you.'

'Lindsay, look at me.'

She brought her chin up with painful slowness. 'Is that what you really thought?'

'What else could I think?'

'You could have thought the truth. You didn't disgust me.'

'But it was on your face. I saw it.'

He shook his head. 'No, Lindsay. I've never thought you were anything but a woman of sheer delight. There's nothing about you that doesn't please me. The disgust you saw was leveled at myself. Did I really say that you disappointed me?'

'Yes, quite definitely,' Lindsay affirmed.

'I'll have to take your word for it. I must have spoken without thinking. What I should have said was that I was disappointed in myself. Except that that's too mild a word to cover how I felt, how I still feel. Are you going to make me tell you, or are you going to be very kind and let me off? I don't come out of this too well.'

'Be fair! You wouldn't let *me* off. But in any case, you can't leave it there. You've got to tell me.'

'That's what I was afraid of. It's a complete mix-up. To begin with I was jealous. Then I was ashamed of my jealousy and lack of understanding. That was followed by the self-disgust I've just spoken of for my overbearing conceit in thinking that I, a comparative stranger, should have taken precedence over the brother you'd known and loved all your life. Of course your first loyalty had to be to Phil's memory. I should have admired you for it, not been jealous of it. But that's only the tip of the iceberg. Your words about having to earn the good things in life struck home. I wanted you, and I thought that was good enough reason to reach out and take you. Not just your body. I wanted the essence of you, your goodness and sweetness and unquestionable devotion and loyalty, without doing anything to earn them. It came to me that I was guilty of all the things I'd accused your brother of, because his crime had also been reaching out and taking what he wanted.'

'And *that's* why you left?' Lindsay gasped in joy.

'That's why. I don't know how I managed it, or how you manage it, for that matter,' Nick choked out.

'Manage what?'

'Light a fire in me that I can't handle. I can't handle talking about it with you so near and desirable.'

She'd been sitting on the backs of her legs; now she strained forward, reaching high enough to brush close to him in a way that made her breasts a magnet for his fingers. As the tips of them glanced over the hard peaks pressing against the bodice of her dress, he said roughly, 'There's more. Don't you want to hear it?'

'Not particularly. I reckon I've heard all I want to know.' She was so happy that she felt light-headed—and mischievous. 'Talking's overrated. I know something better we could be doing,' she said, her fingers taking a walk of their own.

Nick groaned and grabbed hold of her hand. 'You can stop those . . . those . . .' He was searching for the right words, and brought out in triumph, 'wild and wanton tricks. And hear me out. I made up my mind to prove to you that I don't want the fleeting pleasure you dismissed in such derogatory terms. Sure, I wanted to make love to you, not just that night, but every night for the rest of my life and any other time that I get the chance. I wanted—*want*—the lasting happiness you spoke of. You're the best and most worthwhile thing that's ever happened to me, and I knew that I had to start doing something to deserve you. It wasn't something I could bully you into; I had to earn your devotion and eternal love. I'm not going to rush you. That's why I'm not making any business appointments and why I'm canceling the existing ones. I want to give all my time to you in an all-out bid to get you. I'm going to woo you with flowers and all the other romantic trimmings that a woman sets store by.' His voice thickened. 'I love you so much!'

Lindsay's throat was tight. 'Nick, darling, you proved that when you came hurtling to my rescue. You could come weighed down with flowers and chocolates and gifts galore, but you wouldn't look as good to me as you did when I saw your face through that windshield.'

'You mean you're not going to make me prove myself?'

She pressed herself closer to him, delighting in his arousal and the awesome sense of power that flooded through her. Her eyes danced up to his face, eager to soak up every facet of his expression.

'Don't go getting any wrong ideas. *You bet* I'm going to make you prove yourself! You said you walked out on me for a different reason than the one I thought. You say you still fancy me.'

'I do,' Nick declared fervently.

Enjoying herself, warming to the theme, Lindsay then asked, 'And do you desire me to distraction?'

'Oh, yes!'

'And do you want to make wild, passionate love to me?'

'Yes, yes, yes, you wanton, adorable, delightful, delicious woman!'

He had her drift.

'So what are you waiting for? Prove it!' she demanded.

'My pleasure!' he said, his laughter drowning hers as he swept her into his arms.